Bob Moats

I0537642

Fatal
Séance

1

Fatal Seance

ISBN-13: 978-0692319406
For information and address:
Magic 1 Productions
P.O. Box 524, Fraser MI 48026-0524
Website: http://murdernovels.com
Cover by Bob Moats

Extra special thanks to:

Special thanks to Susan Haughton who edited this book and for her great suggestions.

Thanks to the beta readers Cindy Gross Valstad, Al Norris, Carolyn Linington and Amy Morningstar.

Thank you to all the people who purchased this book. I hope you enjoy it as much as I enjoyed writing it for my faithful readers.

The Jim Richards Family of Readers is listed in the back of the book.

Fatal Séance
by Bob Moats

Chapter 1

The gypsy caravan rolled into Brinnon, just after midnight. The crescent moon was not bright enough for them to be seen, but they knew where they were going. They were the advance team to scout out a place to set up the carnival that was following closely behind.

The town council had hired the carnival to celebrate the coming of the autumn festival. It occurred every October just after the first day of fall. This year the council had extra money to hire a bigger carnival to set up and provide fun for all.

The council had hired this carnival on a recommendation from another town in Oregon. Brinnon, Washington had never had a decent carnival before. The ones prior were just basically kiddie rides and sideshows that didn't impress anyone.

This carnival had larger adult type rides that would frighten even the brave at heart. The sideshows were guaranteed to amaze the skeptics of strange science oddities. Real freaks and geeks that would thrust needles through their arms and swallow swords. There was the standard bearded lady and wolf boy, along with the Cardiff giant, a big stone statue that was supposed to have been a real giant at one time.

The advance team exited their travel trailer and walked around the large field, checking to be sure there was enough room for the rides and tents that held the sideshow. They scouted out if there were hook-ups for electricity from power poles, and confirmed if the area was accessible to roads for people to drive in and park.

They felt it was a good place to present their wonder show, and to take a few people captive on their amusements.

~~*~~

Sarah woke up feeling miserable. Van Gogh, her Airedale dog, was standing by her bed watching her struggle to sit up.

Fatal Seance

"Thanks, you miserable animal. Couldn't help me to get up earlier, could you," she said as she lifted her legs over the side of the bed. She looked at the clock on the bed's side table and groaned. "Damn," she said and stood.

Her husband, Dave, sheriff of Jefferson County, where the town of Brinnon was situated, had gone off to protect the town from speeders and litterers.

She usually tried to get up before Dave would leave to go off to work so she could pack him a lunch and kiss him goodbye. This morning she was feeling more miserable than usual. Sarah and Dave had returned last month from their trip to Las Vegas where they renewed their wedding vows. They had help from their friends, Jim and Penny, in getting through the wedding even after bad men had tried to poison people. They stopped them.

Sarah was happy to be back in her own bedroom, even with the sickness she was starting to feel lately. She had a horrible thought, maybe she was pregnant. Not that it was a horrible thing to happen, it was just something she wasn't ready to go through.

She'd have to pick up a pregnancy kit to be sure. It was not something she wanted to do. She knew if she went into the local drugstore and bought a kit, it would be all over town in a matter of hours. Especially if Lois found out, then it would hit the media all the way up to Seattle.

"Come on, dog, I'll get you breakfast. I'm not interested in eating this morning." She looked down at the dog staring back up at her. "Okay, fine, just so you know, I may be pregnant. If you tell anyone, I'll chain you up in the backyard. You understand?"

The dog was wagging its tail and huffing. "Good, we have an agreement. Damn, how do I tell Dave if I am pregnant?"

She went out to the kitchen and poured a bowl of dry food for the dog. He was bouncing around as she set it on the floor. She went back into the bedroom to dress, then came back out to the living room. She stood looking out the floor to ceiling windows at the Hood Canal.

It always was a wonder to her, looking out at the water and remembering the men who died in this room. Two serial killers and one terrorist, who were stopped by Dave along with Warren Stevens and Walt from the FBI. They had replaced the carpeting a few times since the blood stains weren't easy to remove.

Fatal Seance

She was feeling queasy again, and thought she had to get a pregnancy test. She didn't dare ask Dave to pick one up. Then she thought about Virgil, he might be able to get one for her.

Virgil was Dave's deputy and longtime friend. He helped Dave and Sarah a number of times when they were in trouble. Now this was something that she knew would put their friendship to a test.

She picked up the phone and dialed the sheriff's office. She knew that Virgil usually answered the phone, so if Dave answered, she'd just hang up. She waited as the phone rang and finally it was answered, by Virgil. He said, "Sheriff's office, how may I help you?"

"Virgil, this is Sarah, don't say a word, you hear?" she asked him.

He was silent, then Sarah said, "Are you there?"

He said quietly, "You told me not to say anything."

"Good, Virgil. Is Dave nearby?"

"No, he's out by the patrol cars checking the oil," Virgil replied quietly.

"Good, I really need to ask you a terribly big favor. You can't tell Dave about this, you understand?"

"I guess so. Is it some terrible thing, like you're dying?"

"No, Virgil, not that bad. I just need you to do me a favor and go to Davison's Drugs and pick up a couple pregnancy tests for me. Can you do that?"

"What?" he exclaimed loudly.

"Virgil, quiet down," she said louder. "I don't want Dave to know until I see the results. Can you get the tests for me, without giving me away to anyone?"

There was a pause, then Virgil answered. "I think I could do that, but what if someone asks me about why I'm buying them?"

"Say they're for a friend, who you're not going to reveal. You can think of something better, can't you?"

"I guess so. I'll get them and drop them off to you today. You don't want Dave to know?"

"No, I don't. Not until I'm sure. We hadn't planned on children for a while so it's important

9

that he doesn't know, in case I'm not pregnant. Understand?"

"I think so. I'll call when I'm coming to drop them off."

"Thank you Virgil. I'll see you in awhile." She hung up and still felt weird asking him to pick up a pregnancy test. If anyone saw him they would wonder. Virgil had no girlfriend, so it would be strange for him to be buying pregnancy tests.

She turned and found Van Gogh sitting, watching her. "Okay, I feel guilty sending Virgil to get the things, but it would be worse for me to get them. Do you know how fast Lois would organize a baby shower? I don't need that kind of stress," she explained to the dog. "Well, don't just sit there, make me feel better about this."

Van Gogh came over and licked her hand.

*

Chapter 2

Virgil stood as Dave came in the front entrance holding a can of motor oil and a rag. He tossed the can in a trash receptacle by the door and wiped his hands with the rag. He went to the counter and stood looking at Virgil.

"Uh…Dave…uh, I have to run an errand. I'll be back shortly." He rushed out and was gone.

Dave looked at Mike, his other deputy, and said, "That was strange, even for Virgil. I haven't seen him move that fast since the ice cream truck came our way once by accident."

Mike laughed. "He's been a little out of sorts since he got back from his trip with you to Las Vegas. Did he do something wrong out there that he's worrying about?"

"Not that I know of. He had a good time exploring. I didn't keep track of where he went, so maybe he's wanted by LVPD now for something. You may want to check the LEIN to see if there's an arrest warrant out for him," Dave said with a grin.

Fatal Seance

Mike turned to his LEIN monitor and punched the keys on the keypad. Dave laughed, "Mike, I was kidding. I don't think Virgil got in any trouble."

"Oh. Okay, as long as you'll vouch for him," Mike replied. "He got a phone call just before you came in, it might have something to do with that?"

"Do you know who called?"

"No, and he was whispering a lot. Like he was hiding something."

"Well, I'm sure if he wants us to know, he'll tell us," Dave said. "The cars both have their oil checked. One was low, so we have to check more often before we blow an engine. We can't afford a new car, now that the council is spending their entire budget on this carnival they've got coming in this week."

"They hope it will bring in some money to shore up the budget. I'm worried about not having enough police around the place to control the crowds," Mike said.

"I called the sheriff's office in Olympia and asked if they could spare a few officers for a few days. Just until it's over. The carnival is only supposed to be here for three days, I think we can get through that."

"I hope so. Have they come in for permits yet?" Mike asked.

"I haven't any idea. You and Virgil have been here most of the time."

"Well, I haven't seen them apply. They need to get that done before they can set up," Mike said, just as the front entrance doors opened and in came three men, looking like they needed a shower.

Dave turned to them and said, "Can I help you?"

One man came forward and handed Dave some papers. "Here's our application for permits to operate our carnival in the open field west of the town."

"Ah, yes. We were just wondering when you'd be in. Is the field good for your set up?"

"Yes, we are starting to bring our trucks in now, as we speak." The man had an accent that reminded Dave of the way people speak in Slavic countries. He thought of Bella Lugosi in Dracula.

Fatal Seance

"My deputy will take care of the permits. I hope you have a pleasant stay here in our town. Please observe our laws, we don't have a very big jail."

The man laughed. "We very rarely go out into the towns we visit. We are too busy with our operations and maintaining our equipment."

"Sounds like a boring life," Dave replied.

"We have ways of having fun, Sheriff."

"I'm sure you do, sir," Dave said. "Now I have to go patrol, so my deputy will take care of your paperwork."

Mike had stood and went to the counter as Dave handed him the papers. "I'll be back, call if you need me," Dave said to Mike. He smiled at the men and left.

Outside he stood looking around the area. From the sheriff's office, one could see a number of businesses and the Halfway House Restaurant. The park was in front of the office, where kids would play and parents felt safe that they were close to the sheriff's Station.

He walked to the car that was left since Virgil took the other on his unknown mission and got in.

14

He drove out and around to Highway 101 and went by the Brinnon General store. He turned on to Brinnon Lane and went out to the end of the road to the field where the carnival was setting up. The property was privately owned but they had given permission to the town council to use the property. The whole area around Brinnon was mostly forest, so an open bit of land was at a premium.

He sat watching the men scurry around setting up the rides and tents. It always amazed him how they could assemble the rides to do complex maneuvers to twirl, spin, or shake people around. He often wondered if they were really safe to go on. If they weren't, then carnivals would be shut down. He watched men putting together a complex roller coaster ride, wondering if a car would go flying off one day.

He looked in his rear view mirror and saw a couple more large trucks coming down the road. One passed him and had painted in big letters on the side, "Millosovic Amusements and Sideshows" in blazing red and gold.

He always felt like a kid around carnivals and circuses. Ever since his father had taken him to them years ago. Now just a memory. He thought about someday being a father and bringing his kids to the carnival. Maybe he should have a serious talk with Sarah about this, since she was the one who would have to bear the weight of the birth process.

He started the car up and drove back out the road. He thought about driving by the house to see if Sarah had managed to crawl out of bed. He'd do it later, first he had to patrol the town for terrorists or serial killers. He laughed out loud and drove off.

~~*~~

Virgil took a long time sitting in the patrol car trying to build up the nerve to go buy the pregnancy tests. He had told Sarah that he would take care of it, so he had to go in and do it. Then get out fast.

He exited the car and went through the door. He immediately was greeted by a salesgirl he knew and she said hello to him. He felt his face getting red and said a quick hi back.

He scooted over to the pharmacy area and wandered the aisles looking for any pregnancy tests. There were just so many boxes of all kinds of things, it was confusing him. Then he saw them.

He felt relieved that the boxes were small and not obvious for people to see.

He pulled two off the hooks and carried the embarrassing items to the front counter. Luckily there were no other customers standing in line. He went to the counter and found a man at the cash register. He didn't know the man, so he probably wouldn't be embarrassed by any questions. He set the boxes on the counter and the man picked them up to scan.

The man looked at him and said, "Pregnancy tests, eh? For your wife?"

Virgil panicked and said, "No, they're for my mother." He must have turned three shades of red, paid, grabbed the bag and left.

*

Chapter 3

Virgil drove out of the parking lot, just short of using his sirens and flashers to get away. He took a big breath of air and relaxed. He pulled his cell phone and called Sarah.

"I got them and I'm on my way. I need to get back to the office, so I'm just dropping them off," he said and disconnected the call.

Sarah went to the front porch to wait for Virgil. Van Gogh was sniffing around the yard and then saw Virgil pull in. He ran for the car and jumped up on the door as Virgil stopped.

"Van Gogh, get down!" Sarah yelled as she approached the car. The dog moved away and waited to see who was getting out.

Virgil rolled the window down and handed the bag out to Sarah. She smiled and took it.

"How much do I owe you?" she asked.

"It's on me, my treat. Please don't ask me to do that again."

Sarah laughed. "Sorry to have to put you through that. Did anyone see you?"

"No one you need to worry about. Although the guy at the checkout is wondering why my mother needs the tests."

"Virgil! You told him it was for your mother?"

"Won't matter to her. She passed away five years ago. I hope that guy doesn't find out."

"Well, thank you again. If it's good news, you'll be the second person I'll tell, after Dave."

"Thanks, Sarah and good luck." He put the car in reverse and pulled out of the drive.

As he was pulling away, Dave was coming down the highway. He saw Virgil heading out of the drive and wondered why. As he passed Virgil, he could see the man was looking sheepish. He pulled into the drive and up to the house. Sarah had already gone into the bathroom to take the test, so she hadn't seen Dave drive in.

Dave came in the front door and called, "Sarah, what was Virgil doing here?"

Sarah couldn't hear him, she had the bathroom door shut. Van Gogh was sitting outside the door, waiting. Dave came in the bedroom to see the dog sitting there. He approached just as Sarah was opening the door and saw someone in the room. She let out a bloodcurdling scream that could be heard in the next county.

Dave jumped back as Sarah went back into the bathroom slamming and locking the door.

"Sarah. It's me, Dave," he called to her.

"What are you doing here?" she called back through the door. She was hiding the pregnancy stick in the cabinet under the sink. She went to the door and opened it.

"I came by to see if you were all right. What was Virgil doing here?"

"I had him run an errand for me. Don't ask."

"Okay, are you using my deputies to run errands for you now?" he said with a smile.

"Just this one time. It was a personal matter, and I needed Virgil to handle it."

"Will I ever find out?" Dave asked.

"Maybe, it depends, possibly, or maybe not. I'll let you know, or not," she mumbled.

"You are one screwy woman. I guess that's why I love you."

"Got some time to fool around?" she said changing the subject.

"No, I have to get back. The carnival is setting up and I need to be ready for anything. Not that I think there will be problems, but better to be in town than in bed," he said with a grin.

"So, go. I have work to do. I need to work on my latest book about the alien abductions that you, Warren and Walt went through."

"Okay, I may be late, so have dinner without me. I'll call if all is going well enough to get away." He kissed her and went out of the room. Sarah let out a big breath of air when she heard the front door close.

She rushed back into the bathroom and pulled the stick out to check the blue lines. She took a breath and glanced at the small opening that would tell her if she was pregnant or not. She sucked air as she read the results.

She was pregnant.

Fatal Seance

~~*~~

Dave drove back to the office and saw Virgil hadn't returned yet. He parked and went in. Mike was sitting at his desk reading a paper. "Did you get the carnival people all set with the permits?"

"I did. They had all the paperwork made out, so it was easy. Virgil called in and said he was going to catch speeders on the 101."

"Good, we can use the extra fines to cover all the coffee we drink. Any other problems going on in town?"

"Just Ida McIntosh, she called about ten minutes ago to say she had intruders on her property. I was going to call you."

"Were they the zombies she had last time?" Dave said with a grin.

"I thought you said we weren't allowed to mention zombies again."

"You're right, I'm sorry. Now, are the intruders still there, shall I take a ride?"

"She's not sure. She thinks they're hiding in her barn," Mike replied.

"Okay, I'll ride out and check. Let Virgil know where I'm going."

He left the office and went back to the car. He remembered when Ida had called in about the zombies that she killed. They were two men who had a deadly virus that was the beginning of a lot of trouble for them.

He pulled in to the drive of Ida's farm, although it was no longer being farmed since her husband passed away years ago. He wondered why she even kept it. He parked and could see Ida standing at her door with the big shotgun she used to blast the zombies. She waved so he felt safe going towards her.

"I think they're still in the barn. I haven't seen them come out yet," she said through the screen door.

"How many were there?"

"One or two, I didn't get a good look."

"Okay, stay in the house. I'll go look."

"I'll back you up out here, Sheriff Dave."

23

Fatal Seance

Dave was trying not to laugh at the woman's determination to save her land. He came up to the open doors of the barn and called in, "This is Sheriff Chandler, Jefferson County Sheriffs. If you're in there, I'd suggest coming out now. You're trespassing." Dave had his weapon drawn, just in case. He moved over to the side of the opening and looked in. The animals that had been boarded in here were now gone. The barn was cleaned out and empty. The stalls for the horses were still standing and made a good hiding place for intruders.

He stood listening and heard movement. He turned and went around the side of the barn looking in a window where he could see the stalls better. The windows were dirty, and obstructed a clear view, but he could see someone huddling in one of the stalls. Now that he had an idea where the intruder was, he went to the back door and quietly went in.

He snuck around the stalls and came to the one where he saw the person hiding. He looked over the stall next to the person and held his gun on him. "I'd suggest you show me your hands," he said.

The figure huddling brought his hands out and stood. It was a boy of about twelve. "Don't shoot, I'm not armed."

Chapter 4

Dave came around the stall and holstered his gun. "Okay, for starters, who are you?"

The boy was looking scared, so Dave smiled and said, "Let's go sit outside, where we can talk."

They walked out of the barn with Dave holding on to his shoulder, just in case the boy decided to run. Ida saw the boy and came out.

"Ida, leave the shotgun in the house, please," Dave asked.

She returned to the small porch and put the shotgun just inside. Dave took the boy to a couple wooden lawn chairs and had him sit. Ida came over.

"He's just a boy," she said.

"Yes, he is. Now son, you want to tell me your name?"

He hesitated, then said "Gabe Doolard."

Fatal Seance

"Short for Gabriel?" Dave asked.

The boy nodded his head. Dave asked, "Do you live around here? I haven't seen you before."

The boy shook his head no, and said, "I live in Salem, Oregon."

"What are you doing up here? Where are your parents?"

"They abandoned me here. They drove up here and dropped me off."

"Long way to drive to drop you off. Where were they heading?" Dave asked.

"I heard them say Seattle. They were running from the law. After robbing a convenience store in Portland."

"Were you with them when they hit the store?"

"I was in the back seat. They went in and shot the cashier, then ran out. They got to this town and told me to get out."

"Well, this is not a direct route to Seattle. They went a couple hundred miles out of the way to get here. Are you making this up, Gabe?"

The boy went silent. "Okay, Gabe, let's go take a ride," Dave said.

He helped the boy up and took him to the patrol car and put him in the back seat. "Buckle up," Dave said. He turned to Ida, "Thanks for the call. I'll let you know what happens."

She thanked him for coming and went back to her house. Dave got in and made a call to Mike. He came on the radio and Dave said, "I have the intruder. I'll be back in a couple minutes. Call Millie Davis over at County Health and Welfare and ask her to come in." Mike agreed and Dave drove out.

He arrived back at the station and took the boy in. Dave told the boy to sit next to his desk and asked Mike to watch him. He went in the break room and took out a can of Pepsi from the fridge and brought it out to the boy.

The boy thanked him for the Pepsi as Dave sat. "How old are you?"

"Twelve," he replied quietly.

"Okay, I have to wait until a social worker gets here before I can talk to you, since you are under age. So just relax until she gets here."

Fatal Seance

About ten minutes later, a woman in a suit came in. She was in her fifties and fairly attractive. Dave stood and went to her. He explained why he called her and how he found the boy. She followed Dave to the boy and Dave pulled a chair for her over next to him. She sat and said that Dave could question him.

"Gabe, this is Miss Davis, she's a social worker and will act as your guardian for now." Dave sat at his desk. "Now you want to tell me the real story of why you are here? Are you really from Salem, Oregon?"

The boy nodded his head and said, "Yes, I am."

"Okay, I don't think your parents abandoned you, how did you get here?"

"I ran away. I was hiding with the carnival, but they found me in one of the trucks and I had to get away."

"They didn't know you were traveling with them?"

"No, I would climb in one of the trucks after they packed it up and hide until the next town. Then I would sneak out before they found me."

"How did you eat?"

"The food tent would throw out food and I'd go through the trash. They would throw out good food."

"Very resourceful, but dangerous. You could have been hurt traveling that way. Do your parents know you ran away?"

"I was running away from foster care. My parents are not good people."

"Why did you leave the carnival, and end up on the farm property?" Dave asked.

"Those carnival people aren't very nice. They would get drunk and fight. I was getting afraid."

"It's not a life for a child. Miss Davis will provide you with a safe place to stay for the night until we can arrange to find out where your former foster care people went wrong." He stood and said, "Gabe, you can trust us. We won't let you come to harm, that's a promise."

The boy half smiled and stood. Miss Davis took his hand and thanked Dave, then they went out. Dave turned back to Mike, watching the whole incident. "I wonder about our system for taking care of children. It's all messed up."

Virgil came through the door and up to the counter. "Well, the prodigal son returns," Dave said.

"Huh?" Virgil said, not grasping the term.

"Never mind. What were you doing out at my house earlier?" Dave asked.

He hesitated. "I was sworn to secrecy and if I open my mouth I shall be doomed to your wife's wrath. So don't ask," he said.

"That bad, eh? Well, I don't want to bring down wrath from my wife on you. I know what her wrath is like, it's not pleasant. So I'll just wait until she tells me," Dave chuckled. "How did ticket giving go?"

"I nailed fourteen offenders. They just think they can barrel down the 101 and whiz through town without slowing. Well, they all have nice tickets now," Virgil said proudly.

"Good work, Virgil. File the tickets for the court clerk and then go hang around the carnival to keep curiosity seekers away. They're still putting up the rides and tents, so the festival hasn't started yet. We don't want anyone who shouldn't be there getting hurt."

"I can do that," he said, looking like a kid given keys to the candy factory. He went back out to his car, and left.

"Mike, make a call to social services for Salem, Oregon and find out what Gabe was doing in their system. Let me know what you find out," Dave asked.

"I'll get right on it," he said.

"Good," Dave said, and stood watching Mike call.

~~*~~

Sarah was setting the table, hoping Dave would come home at a normal hour so she could make her announcement. She was going to make it a special night, complete with candles and champagne. She had saved the champagne for a special occasion, what could be more special than a baby?

Van Gogh was following her around the rooms that she was flitting between. She was allowing him to get in the way, since she was happy. She would tell Dave about the pregnancy and then she had to call Virgil, she promised him she would let him know.

This was all so strange to her. A baby wasn't something she had ever considered, something that would change her body and life, as well as bringing a new life into this miserable world. She had to be positive and hope for the best for the child she would carry for nine months.

She hoped Dave would be happy, too.

*

Chapter 5

Dave sat at his desk feeling bored. He looked to Mike and asked, "You're on double shift tonight?"

"Yep, I'll be here until you come back in the morning," Mike replied. "Virgil is leaving around eight tonight and will be back tomorrow before noon."

"Well, I'm going to head out. Let Virgil know that I'll see him tomorrow." Dave stood and pulled his cell phone, calling Sarah.

She answered after the first ring. "Were you sitting by the phone?" Dave laughed.

"I was hoping you'd call," she replied. "Are you coming home?"

"I am, feel like going out for dinner?"

"No, I'm making dinner," she answered.

That worried Dave. Sarah wasn't a bad cook, but she wasn't a good cook either.

"Don't worry, it's all pre-packaged foods, I just have to warm them. What time do you think you'll be here?"

He looked at his watch and said, "In about twenty minutes."

"I'll start the food warming process. You should get here before they burst into flames," she laughed and hung up.

Fatal Seance

Crazy woman, Dave thought to himself. He stood and told Mike he was leaving. He went out to his new Range Rover, the one he drove to Vegas, and got in. He arrived at the house and didn't see any smoke, so he figured it was safe to go in.

"Honey, I'm home," he laughed coming in. He took a whiff and it smelled good.

Sarah came bouncing out of the kitchen and led him to the living room. "Sit here until I finish getting the food ready." She handed him a beer that was sitting on the coffee table.

"Well, this is nice. What's the occasion?" he asked.

"You'll find out, now just wait. I have to finish setting up the table." She went back into the kitchen and he could hear her moving plates and silverware around. He waited.

Van Gogh came over and crawled up on the couch next to Dave, he stroked the dog as he rolled over for him. About ten minutes later, Sarah came out and took Dave's hand, pulling him into the dining area.

"Well, this is fancy. I hope the occasion is awesome. Did you get a big advance on your book from your publisher?"

"No, just sit and eat. Then I'll tell you."

"Does this have something to do with Virgil being here today?" Dave asked.

"Will you shut up and eat?" she warned him.

He tried not to laugh aloud and started to eat. The food was good and he finished quickly.

"You eat too fast," Sarah said. "I slaved over this meal and you just wolf it down. Okay, now dessert."

She stood and went out to the kitchen. She came back in with a covered plate, setting it down in front of him. He stared at it and asked, "What's this?"

"Take the cover off and see."

He took the cover and lifted it, placing it next to the plate. He stared at the strange item on the plate. It was a blue and white stick with a small window on the side. "What's this?" he said, then his mouth dropped. He picked up the stick and looked carefully at it.

"Is this what I think it is?" he asked, excitedly.

Fatal Seance

"It is. Virgil picked it up for me today. How do you feel about it? We never discussed children."

Dave put the stick back down and stood, coming around the table to her. He put his arms around her and gave her a big kiss on the lips. He held his head back and said, "Can we still have sex?"

"We better. Don't use this as an excuse to avoid sex," she replied.

"Believe me, it's the last thing on my mind," he said. "That stick says you're pregnant, make an appointment at the clinic to get tested properly. These things are just the first line of info."

"I already called, and I have an appointment tomorrow."

"Good start, now you have to take it easy."

"I'm not fragile, women have carried and birthed babies forever, and many have lived in the wilderness."

"Sure, but you aren't in the wilderness. So I hope you'll cut back on your hectic lifestyle," Dave said hopefully. "When are you going to tell others, like Lois?"

"Oh, hell, no. If she finds out, I'll be plagued with her over here every day. I finally got her to stop bugging me. This will just give her new ammunition."

Dave's cell phone rang and he hesitated. "Answer it. Could be trouble," Sarah said.

Dave let her go and took out his phone, clicking the button. "Hello?" He listened for a moment then clicked off. "That was Mike, they got a call about finding a body north of town beside the highway. Virgil went to investigate and called Mike to say it looks like he was dumped." He went to get his keys from the key rack and said, "You just rest, I'll be back later." He started to go out.

Sarah yelled, "Don't mention the pregnancy yet."

He waved and went out. She went to the screen door to watch him leave. She now had a new reason to worry about him being a cop. Dead bodies mean criminals who could shoot him. She didn't want the baby to be an orphan before it was even born.

~~*~~

Fatal Seance

Virgil was standing by the road waving drivers to keep moving as Dave pulled up and parked behind Virgil's cruiser.

"What's it look like, Virg?" Dave asked as he approached, then saw the body sprawled on the shoulder of the road.

"I'd say he was pushed or thrown out of a vehicle and dumped here. He's close to the road, so they didn't even pull over."

"The shoulder is soft, so the vehicle would have left tire prints. They weren't dumb," Dave said as he knelt down to the body. He carefully turned the man and saw the bullet hole in his side. "Well, this is now a homicide. Call the State Police forensic people and call Doc Norris to come with his crew to examine the body."

Virgil went to his car to get on the radio. Dave stood watching traffic slow to see what was going on. Dave made gestures to keep moving. People can be such ghouls, he thought.

Virgil finally came back and said, "Doc Norris will be here shortly. State Police will send their people down when they can."

"Not much for them to go on. No tire marks, no trace around the body. It's a clean dump, so they can't really get much from this scene. When Doc is finished with his examination, we'll see what the body has on him for ID."

About ten minutes later, a black van pulled up and on to the shoulder. The county medical examiner, Doctor Norris exited the passenger side of the van, being driven by one of his helpers.

He came to Dave and Virgil and said, "Haven't had a good body dump in a while."

"Well, we don't need them. Dump the bodies in Olympia or Seattle, not in our humble little town."

The doctor went to the body and started examining him. He pulled out a wallet from the man's pants pocket and handed it to Dave, after Dave put on rubber gloves. He opened it and went through the various cards and photos. He found the driver's license and read aloud, "Matthew Doolard, Salem, Oregon. Seems I've heard of that last name before?"

*

Chapter 6

"Forensics won't find anything around here. As you said, it was a clean dump," Doc said.

"Find out what you can on the body and let me know," Dave said as the helpers were loading the body in the van. "I had Virgil call the forensic people to cancel the call. They have more pressing scenes to examine."

After the ME van pulled out, Dave turned to Virgil and said, "I have to go see a young man about this body. I'll be in the office later."

Dave went to his Rover and sat, looking through his contacts for Millie Davis' number. He found it, hit the speed dial and waited. She came on the phone and he said, "Millie, this is Dave Chandler. Are you busy?"

"No, Dave, what do you need?"

"I have a strange coincidence regarding Gabe Doolard. Did you place him yet?"

"He's in our temporary shelter for now. He seems to like it. What do you have?"

"I'll tell you when I get here. Keep an eye on him, I'll see you shortly."

They finished and he hung up. Dave looked around the area, Virgil had already left and traffic was back to normal. He pulled out and drove over to the county building where the boy was being kept for now. He went in and knew where to go, he had been there before.

"Dave, you have me curious about what you said on the phone. I checked on Gabe and he's with other children, playing. I'll take you to him."

"I'll need a private room to talk to him, also," Dave requested.

"No problem." They went through the building to a large room with three children playing. Gabe was playing with Legos along with another boy about his age.

Gabe looked over to the door as Dave came in. He stood, went to Dave and waited. "We meet again, Gabe. How are you doing?" Dave asked the boy.

"Good," was all he said.

41

"I need to talk to you, can you follow us please?" Dave said and nodded to Davis. She took them to a room down the hall from the play room.

They entered the room, and Dave asked the boy to sit at the table in the room. Dave and Davis sat across from the boy. He had a look on his face that said he was worried.

"Gabe, I need to know a few things. You said you were from Salem, Oregon, correct?"

The boy nodded.

"Do you know a Matthew Doolard?"

The boy's eyes widened and he started to panic. "He isn't here, is he?" Gabe said excitedly.

"Why does that worry you?" Dave asked.

"He wants to hurt me. He's an uncle, my father's only brother and he hates me. It's one of the reasons I ran away. He wanted to take me out of foster care and he would have beaten me."

"Wouldn't your parents object to him having you?"

"My father is in prison and my mother is in a drug treatment hospital, she doesn't care about me," he said quietly.

"Why would your uncle want to take you?" Dave asked.

"He can make money off me from the state. Welfare would pay him to take care of me."

"How do you know this?"

"I heard him talking to some man who was with him when he came to the foster care house I was in. He was asking them if he could take me, but the people I lived with said they'd have to talk to social services. He was mad and went away saying he'd be back. That's when I left. The carnival was in town and I hid in one of their trucks."

"So he wasn't good to you?"

"No, he treated me like crap when he would come to the house my mom had before they arrested her for drug possession and I was taken by the state."

Dave wondered if he should tell Gabe the man was dead. He may know something that may help in the investigation, so Dave said, "Gabe, I have something to tell you. We found Matthew Doolard's body on a road north of town. He was murdered." Dave waited to see what reaction he would get.

The boy was silent for a moment then said quietly, "Good."

"Do you know why he may have been killed?" Dave asked.

"Probably drugs," Gabe said. "He and my mom would do drugs together and she got busted, but he didn't."

"Why would he come all the way up here to find you?"

The boy was silent again. Dave waited, as he looked like he didn't want to say why.

"Take your time, I'd just like to find out who murdered him," Dave said.

"I took a bunch of his drugs in a briefcase and brought them with me," he said softly.

Dave sat back, amazed at this revelation. "How did you get the drugs?"

"One night he came to the foster care home and grabbed me. He took me to his house and beat me." Gabe raised his shirt and showed them a couple of bruises. "He was getting high with some guy and I went in his room and took the briefcase and left the house. That's when I went with the carnival."

"Well, this is getting deep. Anything else you want to tell us? Truthfully now."

"I was found by some guy in the carnival here in this town and he took the briefcase. I was going to use the drugs to make money to live on. He held me in a trailer and kept asking me where I got the drugs. I had to tell him about my uncle, I was afraid he would kill me if I didn't. He said he was going to call my uncle and work a deal with him for the drugs and me. When he went to call, that's when I slipped out and ran to that woman's barn."

"Well, you're safe now from your uncle. I need to find this person in the carnival. I may need your help in identifying him. Think you can do that?"

The boy nodded and Dave said, "I'll get back to you. I have to arrange a few things first. Can you stay here for now, you won't run away again?"

"No, I feel safe here, thank you," he said.

"Okay, I'll be back. Hang in there, it will get better." Dave stood, thanked Millie Davis and left.

Back out at his vehicle, he sat thinking. What a mess for the boy. There was someone in the carnival who may have killed the uncle for the drugs. It fit. The uncle must have come up from Salem, to make a deal and they killed him. He felt he needed help on this, maybe call in Warren Stevens and the FBI. Interstate transport of drugs to sell, but he didn't want the boy to get in trouble. He had to tread lightly.

He started the car and drove out. He arrived back at the station and found Virgil at the desk.

"Where's Mike?" Dave asked.

"We switched shifts. I had nothing to do tonight, so he left."

"Okay, I have a call to make, don't let anyone disturb me," he said and went into the break room, closing the door. He dialed a number and waited.

"Warren, Dave here. I think I may need your help."

*

Chapter 7

"Speak to me, oh great sheriff. I am your humble servant," Warren said over the phone.

"I got a kid here that may be involved in drugs and murder. The kid is a pawn in this story, so we have to keep him safe."

"Okay, explain."

Dave told him the whole story from when he found the boy hiding, to the revelation of murder and drugs.

"Well, it's not a couple of serial killers or a terrorist with a deadly virus. Your crimes are getting boring. Drugs and murder are everywhere, but what you have is interesting. Why do you need my help? Are you afraid of a few carnies?"

"Warren, you know Mike and Virgil are good cops, but I worry about something like this. I don't want to deal with carnies who murder."

"If they did it. You don't know yet."

"Very true, but if I take the boy into their lair to ID the guy who took the drugs, I worry for his safety."

"You have a gun, use it," Warren laughed through the phone.

"I'm calling for back-up. Are you in?"

Warren was quiet for a moment. "What's in it for me?"

"You get a nice place to sleep and home cooked meals."

"Are you cooking or Sarah?" he laughed.

"On another note, you get to celebrate with us. Sarah is pregnant."

"What!" he yelled. "You are capable of getting her pregnant or did you go to a sperm bank?"

"Hey, it's all me, thank you. Now, are you in?"

He thought a moment, again. "I'll talk to my SAIC and see if he doesn't have a problem with it. I'll tell him it's a drug running operation between states. I hope this uncle had more of an investment in this."

"Let me know," Dave said.

"If he says no, I'll take a vacation. So, I'll be there one way or another, probably tomorrow. Oh, and you will name the baby after me if it's a boy." He laughed and hung up.

Dave left the break room and went to the counter. "Any word from Doc about the body?"

"He hasn't called yet. I'll be sure to let you know when he does."

"Thanks, Virgil. I'm going back home. Since you picked up the pregnancy tests, you know about Sarah possibly being pregnant?"

"She told you I got them?"

"She did, and the results were good. Just don't spread that," Dave asked.

"Well, that's just really great. I'm happy for the two of you."

"Thanks, I'll see you in the morning," he said and went out.

He felt a thrill on the way home. He never thought much about children before. At least not actually having one. Or two. Damn, he thought, what if they had twins? One step at a time, he told himself as he pulled into the drive.

Van Gogh came barreling over to him, almost knocking him down. "Hey, dog. What are you doing out here?" he said, just as Sarah came around the corner of the house.

"Hi, hon. We were just out getting some fresh air. I'm trying to settle my stomach, so be ready for many sick mornings."

"I didn't think about that. Do you feel you'll have a rough time of it?"

"I may, I'll see. Let's go in, it's getting chilly out here. Come, Van Gogh, in the house," she commanded.

"So, how was your day?" she asked.

"Very busy," he said, seeing she had cleaned off the table. "I can bore you with details of a trespasser, a runaway boy and a dead body."

She smiled at him and took his hand. She led him in the living room and had him sit on the couch. She told him to wait, went into the kitchen and came back with a can of beer. She handed it to him, sat and said, "go."

He told her all about Ida calling with trespassers, who turned out to be a young boy. He told her about the boy's story and then about the dead body found on the side of the road.

"Turned out the dead man was Gabe's uncle. We're still trying to find out what happened, but I called Warren and he's coming over from Seattle to help investigate."

"Warren is coming?" Sarah exclaimed. "When?"

"He said he'd try to be here tomorrow. I hope so, before the trail of the dead man goes cold."

"Did you mention to him our happy news?"

"I did, and he wants us to name the baby after him, if it's a boy," Dave said with a grin.

"Sorry, but Warren is a good name for him, but not for our baby boy."

"We'll think of names later, but for now I have to get some sleep. The festival starts tomorrow and I have deputies coming from Olympia to help patrol the crowds. I need to be in early. You don't have to get up with me, I understand."

"You just don't want to see me get sick, right?"

51

Fatal Seance

"That was not on my mind. I just want you to rest now. I can make my own lunch or eat out. Either way, you stay in bed."

She didn't argue, she was feeling a little ill already. They went into the bedroom, undressed and got into bed. Dave kissed her and then they snuggled.

Early the next morning Dave had gone out to work as Sarah lounged in bed. She turned to Van Gogh sitting by the bed watching her.

"I hope Dave fed you, because I'm not getting up," she said to the dog. "I could get to like this, sleeping in."

The dog huffed, ran in a couple circles and bounced a couple times. "I get it. He didn't let you out to do your business. Damn, I'll let you out." She threw back the covers and got up as Van Gogh was bouncing out in the hallway now. He shot off for the back door facing the Hood Canal.

Sarah threw on a robe and came out. She opened the door and the dog took off. Sarah laughed when he startled two squirrels chattering to each other. They both shot up a tree as Van Gogh watered the bushes.

She turned and went into the kitchen for a glass of water. She drank the liquid, then felt it coming back up. She rushed for the bathroom and made it in time. She spent a few minutes at the toilet, then went to let the dog back in.

"I'm going back to bed, dog. If you need anything, too bad. You're on your own." She went back into the bedroom and closed the door.

~~*~~

Dave had arrived at the station and found three new deputies standing in the lobby.

"Good morning, deputies," he said. "Follow me, please."

They went into the office as Virgil was getting some coffee from the new machine they bought.

"Virgil, I want you to run point with the men, just like we've done in years past. You can explain the layout to them and get them set up on the grounds of the festival." Dave knew Virgil liked to be in charge, so he always gave him the duty.

Virgil took the men out through the front to take them to the festival grounds and get them ready. Dave sat at his desk and looked through the overnight logs that Virgil posted. Nothing much happened, no crimes, break-ins or shootings. A nice, quiet night.

The front doors opened again, and Dave heard a familiar voice. "The Calvary has arrived."

It was Warren Stevens.

*

Chapter 8

Warren came up to the counter and gave Dave a big grin. "I convinced my SAIC to let me come down here to bust up a big drug ring. He said it wasn't our jurisdiction, so I told a white lie and said there was a young boy kidnapped across state lines, which made it our case. Since Seattle FBI division covers most of the state, you fall into our jurisdiction."

"It's good for the FBI that you didn't become a criminal," Dave said and stood, going to the counter. They shook hands as Dave said, "Did you bring Walt?"

"Nope, he's working surveillance on a terrorist cell. I haven't seen him for about a week, and I'm starting to miss the little guy."

"That's because he did a lot of your work. You're such a con man," Dave said.

"Guilty. Now where is this young boy who we need to identify the suspect?"

"I'll call over there to make sure he's available. He's in the system for CPS." Dave said and pulled out his cell phone.

"I never liked Child Protective Services. They break up families for stupidly thin reasons on the word of people who should keep their noses out of other people's business. But, I'll admit, they do some good."

"Yes, they do, especially when children are being abused. Hold on while I call." He dialed the number for Millie Davis again and waited. He explained that he was bringing a friend to talk to Gabe. She agreed and they ended the call. Dave called Virgil and said he was going out, and told him to come back to watch the station. Virgil said he was on his way already.

"Shall we go?" Dave said. They went out just as Virgil was driving up.

"Hey, Virg, how's tricks?" Warren asked him.

"Good, Agent Stevens," he said back. "Dave, I got the men posted around the festival. It's already got a good size crowd. Lots of rides and attractions."

"Nice. Virgil, we'll be back in a while. Hang on here until Mike gets here, tell him to catch the phones. I'll need you back later tonight to patrol the crowd." Virgil agreed and went in the building.

Dave and Warren went to Dave's car and drove out. They arrived at the county building and went in. Millie had Gabe in the same room as before. He was playing with a toy police car on the table.

She brought Dave and Warren in after Dave introduced them. Gabe smiled at the sight of Dave and sat up.

"Hey, Gabe, long time no see," he joked. Gabe laughed, as everyone sat.

"Gabe," Dave started, "this is a friend of mine, Special Agent Warren Stevens. He's with the FBI and he's going to help us find the man who may have hurt your uncle."

"Murdered my uncle, you mean," the boy said, surprising everyone.

"Well, that's true. Glad you understand. Now, I'd like you to tell Agent Stevens about what happened when you were found at the carnival by the man who took the drugs."

The boy ran the toy police car on the table as he spoke. He told Warren about the incident in detail. Warren was listening to the boy as he talked, and then finished the story.

"That's all I can tell you. I ran from the truck and found the barn to hide in," Gabe said.

Warren asked, "Do you think you can remember what the man looked like? Could you identify him?"

"Sure, I couldn't forget him, he was evil looking, and smelled bad," Gabe replied.

"We just have to identify him by sight, not smell," Warren said with a laugh. "I'm good to go.

When do you want to catch the guy?" Warren asked Dave.

"The festival started this morning so we can't round up all the carnies for a line-up," Dave said. "Maybe if we take Gabe to the carnival and walk around, he may see the man."

"Works for me," Warren said.

"Gabe, would you like to go to the carnival and go on some rides this time? No hiding."

The boy put the car aside and said, "I'd like that. I never was allowed to go to a carnival."

Dave looked at Millie. "Can we take him or do you need to go along?"

"What? Pass up a chance to go to the carnival? I'm going along whether I have to or not," she said with a laugh. "Let's get Gabe ready to go. I'll get his jacket." She went off as Dave stood.

"Gabe, this could be dangerous. We don't know if the man who discovered you in the truck is the killer, but we'll be carefully watching for him. If I tell you to go with Miss Davis, you stick by her."

"Will you arrest the man?" he asked.

Warren answered. "We'll take him into custody to be questioned. If you say he's the man who held you, we can arrest him for false imprisonment and child endangerment. Either way, if we find him, he will be taken in for questioning."

Gabe went silent, then Millie came back with his jacket. He stood and put it on, then everyone went out to Dave's patrol cruiser.

They arrived at the grounds for the festival and parked in the area where the other deputies had their cars. They got out and went to the entrance. There was a small admission fee for the festival, but they got waved through by the people at the entrance. They were local citizens who wanted to help with the festival and knew Dave and Millie Davis.

Dave turned to Gabe and said, "Now pay attention to the men who work on the rides. Don't be afraid, we'll protect you. If you see him, let me know. Now, what ride would you like to go on first?"

The boy's eyes brightened and he pointed to the Ferris wheel.

Dave turned to Millie, "Why don't you go on it with him? I'm paying."

"I'd like that, thank you," she replied and they went to the ride. Dave bought the tickets and Gabe went to where they were loading people. Millie took Gabe's hand as they were seated on the gondola that would take them high above the festival.

"Pretty good crowd for so early in the day," Warren said.

"The locals don't have much to do otherwise," Dave said with a laugh. "Plus the campground folks all come to enjoy the rides, too. Tourists driving through town see the signs the council had erected and they come over also. It'll be more hectic later in the day. I'll have both Virgil and Mike patrolling the grounds in addition to the deputies from Olympia."

"Long shift for them," Warren said.

"Sure, but they are getting overtime pay, so I'm sure they don't mind."

They watched as the big wheel started to rotate and they could see Gabe looking delighted. So was Millie. Dave was looking around at the crowd and could see the deputies moving through the people.

60

Just their presence at the festival helped to keep trouble in check.

Dave grabbed Warren by the arm and pointed. Warren looked back and saw Sarah with Lois.

"Wait here," he told Warren and went to the women. Sarah saw him and grinned.

"What are you two doing here?" Dave asked.

"Why wouldn't we be here? It's a carnival. We can have fun, too," Sarah replied. "Besides, Lois found out they had a fortune teller in the sideshow and since she believes in that stuff, she brought me along."

"Dave, you should get your fortune read. It's amazing how much they know," Lois said.

"I'm here on official business, so I can't indulge in the fun stuff," Dave replied.

"Looking for the uncle's killer?" Sarah asked.

"Yep," Dave said as Warren, Millie and Gabe came up.

"Dave, Gabe spotted the man," Warren said.

*

Chapter 9

"Where?" Dave asked.

"Gabe said he saw the man walking through the crowd from the wheel, but lost sight of him," Warren said.

"At least we know he's here," Dave turned to Sarah. "You and Lois have a nice time. We have a manhunt to do." Dave bent down to Gabe and asked, "What direction was he going?"

Gabe looked back at the Ferris wheel and then thought. "He was going away, in that direction." He pointed and Dave looked that way.

"Okay, we'll work that end now." Dave kissed Sarah and they went off to find the man.

Lois turned to Sarah, "Shall we go see what the fates have in store for us?"

Sarah was trying to please the woman. She didn't believe in all that nonsense of fortune telling. Lois had shown up at Sarah's front door and Sarah opened it before seeing who it was. Lois told her about the fortune teller and wanted her to come with her. She didn't want to go alone to the festival, so Sarah agreed, reluctantly.

Lois was acting like she was forty years younger than her fifty-nine years. They weaved through the crowd and came to the big sideshow tent. The fortune teller had her own tent just off the side of the big tent, looking strange being so isolated.

Lois rushed over and there was a short line to the opening. "Only two people ahead of us. Not too bad," Lois said. 'So what's new with you and Dave?"

Sarah wasn't going to mention the pregnancy. She went in earlier that morning to the clinic and had a test performed. They said she was definitely in her third month already. She was surprised that she was that far along, before they even went to Las Vegas to get re-married. She never kept track of her time of the month, and hadn't thought about missing her periods. That should have given her some clue.

"Oh, good, one more to go, then us," Lois bubbled like a teenager. Sarah had to keep a laugh to herself.

Fatal Seance

A baby name was keeping her preoccupied most of the trip to the festival. She ran through names for boys and girls and couldn't settle on one or another. But then she'd have to discuss that with Dave.

"We're next," Lois announced happily.

The young couple that was ahead of them came out of the small gaily decorated tent. It looked like something out of a medieval story book. Lois led the charge into the tent, followed by Sarah.

The interior was just as medieval as the outside. There were candles burning all around the tent, worrying Sarah. She hoped the tent was fire resistant.

There was an elderly woman dressed in gypsy refinement sitting at a cloth covered table. In the middle of the table was the standard crystal ball. The woman had tarot cards stacked in front of her and she motioned for the women to sit.

The woman's face was deeply wrinkled and she had moles in three places. Sarah tried not to stare at the moles, so she looked to the woman's nose. It wasn't much better than the moles, but she tried not to stare.

The woman held out her hand and said, "Ten dollars, please."

Sarah thought that was a bit excessive, but Lois pulled a ten from her purse and paid the woman.

"Now take the cards and cut them," the gypsy said, handing the tarot cards to Lois.

Lois cut the cards and stacked them back. The gypsy took the cards and broke them into four piles. She took cards from the top of each pile and set them in order, face up. She was studying them and said, "You are a bright woman, you make people happy providing them with shelter."

"Yes," Lois beamed. "I sell real estate."

"Yes, a realtor, you are," she continued. "You have many friends and acquaintances in your life. You will make many more." She turned up a few more cards and spoke, "I see money coming into your future, a lottery perhaps or an inheritance. It will be enough to fulfill your dreams of travel."

"Oh, I love to travel," Lois was excited now. Sarah was not impressed so far.

"You will meet a man in your future, who will wine and dine you, but only for your money, so beware."

"Oh, no." She was crushed now.

"Watch out for strangers who will be friendly to you. They are not what you think."

"I'll be careful," Lois answered.

The old lady turned a few more cards and said, "You'll live a long life, and you'll settle quietly in your hometown with many friends around you." She sat back and continued, "That's all I see, thank you."

"Sarah, you need your fortune told now," Lois said and pulled another ten from her purse, handing it to the gypsy.

"Lois, you don't have to do that," Sarah protested.

"Nonsense, just cut the cards," Lois said as the gypsy had stacked them back up and handed the cards out to Sarah. She stared at the cards, then took them to please Lois. She cut them once and handed them back to the woman.

The gypsy did the same routine of laying out the cards, but she took a little longer with her reading them. Sarah was wondering what the gypsy saw that made the old woman frown.

She was shaking her head, making strange noises from her throat. "I see tragedy and unhappiness. I see a great loss in your future. The loss of a child."

Sarah was shocked at this statement. "What are you talking about," Sarah demanded. "I have no children."

"I'm sorry, it's in the cards. You will lose a child," the old woman spoke quietly.

Sarah yelled, "Nonsense!" and she stood up and stormed out of the tent. Lois was surprised and followed.

"Why did you that? Why did you let her tell me that terrible thing?" Sarah yelled at Lois.

"Sarah, I didn't know she was going to say that. I'm sorry. But as you said, you don't have any children."

"Lois, you didn't know! I'm pregnant!" Sarah started to cry and walked away from Lois. The woman stood looking shocked.

Fatal Seance

~~*~~

Dave and Warren followed the boy as he made his way through the crowd watching for the man. They came out to a ride where the boy stopped and turned to Dave.

"That's him. The man on the side of the ride talking to a woman."

They looked in the direction the boy pointed and saw him. "Millie, stay here with Gabe," he said and motioned to Warren to follow.

The men went to the couple, still talking. The man turned his head and saw Dave in his sheriff's uniform and got a panicked look. He turned to run as Dave ran after him with Warren hot on his heels.

They ran between the trucks used to haul the rides and then back to where the carnival had a tent set up to feed the workers. The man ran in the tent, followed closely now by the men. Dave managed to tackle the man over a table and down to the ground. Warren came up and grabbed the man's arms and they pulled him up. Warren held his badge up as other carnies were now standing wondering why their coworker was being attacked.

"FBI," He yelled. "Back up, we are arresting this man, none of anyone else's business."

The men gave them plenty of room as Dave said to the man, "This isn't your day, is it?"

*

Chapter 10

Lois found Sarah standing by Lois' car, composing herself.

"Sarah, I'm really sorry about what the woman said. I didn't know that you were pregnant."

"It's all right, Lois. I wasn't sure until this morning when I went to the clinic. But why would that woman say those horrible things? Isn't this supposed to be for entertainment, not scaring the hell out of people? She should be shut down."

Fatal Seance

"I agree now. I like to have my fortune told and I read the horoscopes, but I don't really believe in all that. Don't take what she said to heart. I'm sure you'll be all right."

"I'm going to be especially careful now. I'll show that bitch she was wrong," Sarah said, finally breaking a smile. "Can you take me home now, please?"

"Sure, get in and I'll drop you off."

Sarah got in and said, "I don't want my pregnancy going any further than us, please."

"My lips are sealed," Lois said and started the car.

~~*~~

Dave and Warren dragged the man out of the tent and over to the side where the trucks were parked. They handcuffed him to a truck and Dave said, "I'll get Millie and Gabe, just to be sure."

Warren stood staring at the man while waiting.

"What are you looking at?" the man grumbled.

"A piece of crap, if you must know," was all Warren said.

A few minutes later, Dave came back with Gabe and Millie. Gabe was holding on to Millie tightly. The man saw Gabe and looked shocked.

"Gabe, take a look and tell me, is this the man who took the briefcase of drugs and held you captive?"

Gabe looked around Millie at the man and nodded. Dave asked, "Tell me with your own words Gabe, is he the man?"

Gabe said, quietly, "Yes, he's the one."

"Good," Warren said. "You sir, are under arrest for drug possession and imprisoning a minor child. You are also under suspicion for the murder of Matthew Doolard."

The man looked even more shocked, but said nothing.

Warren released the cuff from the truck and put it on the suspect's free wrist.

Fatal Seance

"Let's go around the festival, not through it," Dave said. He called the station to see if Virgil was still there. Mike answered, and said Virgil was just leaving.

"Stop him and tell him to come to the festival. I have a small job for him." Dave hung up and they walked around the fence that was put up to prevent people from not paying the admission. They got back to the car and put the suspect in the back.

"I'm going to have Virgil escort Millie and Gabe around the carnival, to take in a few more rides, then have him take them back to the county building," he told Warren. "We'll take our friend here back to the station and interrogate him."

A few minutes later, Virgil drove up to the cars and parked. Dave told him, "I need you to take Millie and Gabe around the festival and go on a few more rides. Then take them back to the county building shelter."

Virgil looked happy at the prospect of roaming the rides. Dave gave him some extra money and then he and Warren left.

"Do you have the bamboo shoots for under his nails and waterboarding equipment handy?" Warren asked with a grin as they drove the suspect back.

"I think just the rubber hose will do," Dave replied.

"You can't do that," the man said nervously from the back.

Warren looked back at him through the steel mesh panel between the front and back seats and said, "I can do anything, I'm FBI."

They arrived at the station and took the man into a room off the side for questioning people. They sat him down and cuffed him to the table. "Mike, anything pressing at the moment?" Dave called out.

"No, chief. All's quiet here."

"Good, we'll be interrogating our prisoner." Dave closed the door as Warren sat across from the man. Dave sat and looked at the wallet they removed from his pants pocket. He handed it to Warren.

"Melvin Klein, it says on your license. From Tallahassee, Florida. You travel with the carnival, Mel?" Warren said.

Fatal Seance

The man nodded. "I work on the tilt-a-whirl," he said quietly. He was acting awful meek for a killer, Dave thought.

"You saw the boy. He identified you as the man who took a briefcase from him. It had drugs in it. What did you do with it?" Warren asked.

"I was holding it, the boy shouldn't have had it. He told me it belonged to his uncle. The boy gave me his name and where I could reach him. I went to call the man, and when I came back the boy was gone. I just wanted to return the boy and his merchandise to his uncle, that's all."

"Were you trying to shake down the uncle for money in return for the drugs and the boy?"

The man went silent, they waited. "I may have thought that. Hey, it would have been an easy buck. I wasn't going to hurt the boy, and I didn't want the drugs. Too much trouble I could get in holding that stuff. I called the uncle and he said he'd be right up. I didn't know where the boy went to, but I figured the man wanted his drugs more than the boy, or so he said. He arrived with another man and I asked for the money. They both got out of their van and the other man had a gun. He pointed it at me and said to forget the money, just give them the drugs. I didn't need the grief, so I gave it to them. They left and I had nothing for my troubles."

"They came in a van? What did it look like? Describe it," Dave asked.

"It was a late model Dodge van, all white and rusting badly. The man with the gun was driving, the uncle, Doolard, was the passenger. They took the brief case and drove off. That was the last I saw of them, the briefcase or the boy. Until you brought him to the carnival."

Dave stood and asked Warren to follow him. They went out of the room and Dave turned to Warren. "I'm wondering if this second man may have shot Doolard and pushed him out of the van on the highway. It would make sense, he wanted the drugs. This guy doesn't even have a car to take Doolard out to dump. He travels in a semi-truck."

"I hate to say it, but it does make sense. What shall we do with Melvin?"

"From what Gabe told me, Melvin didn't hurt him. It was just like he said. Melvin went out to call Doolard and they came to get the drugs. Double cross happens a lot with drug dealers. Maybe we should turn Melvin loose?"

"I'm not seeing anything that says he's lying. He held Gabe to keep him, while he called Doolard to return him, so he wasn't imprisoned. Gabe managed to get away easily enough. I think we need to run at this from another aspect. The partner who came with Doolard. If I had Walt here I could have him make up a sketch of the suspect."

"I can call Olympia and have a sketch artist here pretty quickly." Dave said.

"Let's do that. I'm sure that will make Melvin happy."

*

Chapter 11

They went back into the room and sat. "Melvin, I have to ask something, why did you run when you saw us?"

"I didn't know what you wanted. When I see cops coming towards me, I panic. I wasn't sure if Doolard turned me in. So I ran."

"Well, now you know Doolard is dead, and we'd like to nab his partner, but we don't know what he looks like. So I'm having a sketch artist come in to have you tell him what he looks like."

"I can help with that." Melvin pulled out his cell phone and did something on it. "I took a sneaky picture on my phone when they got there. I take pictures of women in the midway when they are good looking or wearing sexy clothing." He turned the phone to Dave and Warren. They could see the two men in the van looking at Melvin. "They had just gotten there and didn't see me push the photo button from my pocket."

Dave reached out and took the phone. "Would you send this here to the office? I'll give you our email address."

"Sure, be happy to. Just to get me off this charge," he said hopefully.

Dave looked at Warren, "I guess this backs up his story. Nice photo." Warren took the phone and studied it. "Yep, looks good, nice resolution." He handed the phone back for Melvin to forward the photo.

A few minutes later Dave checked the email and found the photo. He had Mike print out a number of copies.

Fatal Seance

"Melvin, we're trusting that you're telling the truth. So you can go back to the festival. I'll have my deputy take you." Before Dave took the cuffs off him, he snapped a photo of Melvin with his phone.

"For our scrapbook," Dave said with a smile. "Mike, take Mr. Klein back to the festival, please."

Mike came over and led Melvin out. Dave sat at his desk looking at the photo of the men in the white Dodge van. "Good shot of them. Would have been better if they were out of the van standing so we could get a full body shot."

"I'll shoot this email back to our lab and have them run facial recognition on both of them. We know the passenger was Doolard, but it would be good to be sure," Warren said.

Dave got the address from Warren, and sent the email. Warren made a call to the lab to explain the photo. He hung up and said, "Well, we may have a result if the guy is in the system."

"If he's into drugs, I'd say he is. Unless he's very clever," Dave said as the office phone rang. "Jefferson County Sheriff's office, Sheriff Chandler speaking," he said when he answered it. He listened and asked a couple questions then hung up.

"That was Bayside Resort Motel. They are just up the road a little from where we found the body. Seems they have a security camera in the parking lot, because they've had a number of break-ins. The manager was going over the video and he was watching us when we were fussing over the body. He ran the video back until he saw a white van stop just around where we found the body. It pulled away and then he could see the body. We now have verification on who killed Doolard."

~~*~~

Lois pulled into the drive at Sarah's and parked.

"Would you come in and keep me company for a little while?" Sarah asked Lois.

"Yes, I would," she replied and they got out of the car. Sarah opened the front door and was greeted by Van Gogh. He was bouncing around, so she took him out to do his business. Sarah and Lois sat on the porch, watching the dog chase squirrels, finally stopping to water a bush.

Fatal Seance

The women were quiet for a moment then Sarah spoke. "I wanted children during my first marriage. But when he was murdered and I moved out here from New York, I never thought about it. Dave and I never spoke about it. Then I started getting sick and wondered if I could be pregnant. The stick told me I was but the clinic verified it."

"How far along are you?" Lois asked.

"They told me three months. It was the last time I could remember having my period. But it just seems so long ago. I was so happy, but this gypsy woman screwed that up."

"Never mind her, Sarah. Those people have canned scripts they go by, they can all fit most people. I highly doubt I'll ever hit the lottery, I don't buy tickets. I have no rich relatives to leave me money, and I'm not interested in a relationship with a man."

Sarah gave her a look, wondering what she meant by that.

"No, I'm not a lesbian, Sarah," she laughed, noticing the stare. "I'm just not interested in a relationship this late in my life. Too much trouble. I was married once and we had a daughter. I rarely see her, she's somewhere in Georgia. My husband and I never could see eye to eye, so we ended it.

My daughter blamed me for the break-up. I could never sway her to the truth that her father was a creep. So I gave up."

"I'm sorry, Lois. That must have hurt," Sarah said.

"Oh, I've gotten over it. Easy to do when you throw yourself into your work. Why do you think I sell so many homes? I keep busy."

Sarah's phone rang, she went to answer. "Hello?"

"Sarah, it's me," Dave said in her ear. "How was your trip to the festival?"

"I need to talk to you when you get home."

"Sounds serious. Did you go to the clinic and what did they say?"

"They say I'm three months into the pregnancy. They want to send me to Olympia for more tests and scans to see how the baby is doing."

"We can do that. I need to talk to you about having the pitter patter of medium sized feet in our home."

Sarah was silent for a moment. "What?"

Fatal Seance

"Next week is Halloween. There's a young boy in the shelter and there's no one to take him into a foster home. They're all filled according to Millie Davis. I thought we could let him stay with us for a short while during the holiday until they find a more permanent place."

"Are you talking about the boy you found in Ida's barn?"

"That's the one. He's a really good kid, just had a bad life. Parents in prison and rehab, uncle was a drug dealer, murdered this week, and he has no place to go. I thought we could give him a home base for a few days. Just for Halloween."

"Come home and we'll talk about it. I'm a little upset about something that happened at the festival. I'll tell you about it when you get home."

"Okay, I have some investigating to do. I'll call before I come home. Warren will be with me."

"I'll see you then," she said and hung up. She thought maybe this would be a good thing. Having a child in the house may make her feel better.

*

Chapter 12

Dave hung up and Warren asked, "How's our girl doing?"

"I'm not sure, she sounded strange on the phone. Something was bothering her. She said we'd talk about it when I got home. I hope it's nothing serious."

"The *Feminine Mystique*, a book by Betty Friedan. That started a second wave in feminism. Screwed up many men, I'll tell you."

"I don't think Sarah is into feminism. She not radical enough. I guess I'll find out when I get home."

Warren's cell phone buzzed and he looked at the caller ID. "Well, it's Walt," he said and answered. "Hey, junior, where are you?" He put the phone on speaker.

"I'm looking at the photo image you sent to the lab. I came back in to have some video copied and saw your email. I helped Mick run the facial recognition and we got a hit fairly quick. Got something to write on?"

Dave passed him a pad and pen. "Shoot."

"Wilber Rothberg, age 37, last reported he was residing in Salem, Oregon. No address on file presently. He moves around a lot. He has a rap sheet a mile long, from grand theft auto to attempted murder. He's definitely a bad guy. Recently released from prison, paroled. Maybe his parole officer would have a present address. The other man is Matthew Doolard, age 34, address in Salem, also. No record. From your note, he is now listed as deceased. What do you want me to do with this info?" Walt asked.

"Send it to my email address. I'm going to contact the Portland, Oregon, FBI office to see if they can track Rothberg down. He's wanted for the murder of Doolard." Warren said. "How much longer are you going to be on surveillance?"

"We've just about wrapped up our investigation. I just have to file a whole bunch of reports and catalog my videos, then I'll be finished."

"So, a couple days, weeks, months? Will I have my partner back eventually?"

Walt laughed, "Couple days, I'll work fast. Do you need me over there?"

"I always need you, Walt. You keep me in line and out of trouble. Work fast and get here." Warren laughed and hung up. "That should get his adrenaline moving."

"You should be ashamed of the way you treat him," Dave said with a grin.

"Hey, he has it easy working with me. I know how valuable his brain is, so I treat him well."

"Okay, are you going to call Portland FBI and have them track down this Rothberg?" Dave asked.

"I have a friend down there that can get this started. I have to get a warrant for Rothberg's arrest started, so give me a little phone time, then we can go bother Sarah."

"I have to call Millie and see about taking Gabe for a week or two," Dave said.

"Don't make any promises until you talk to Sarah," Warren warned.

Dave considered that. "I guess you're right. So make your calls and let's get moving."

Fatal Seance

Forty minutes later, Warren had his warrant and alerted Portland FBI. The man hunt was beginning.

"Now we can go see how Sarah is doing," Warren said. "I'll follow you in my car."

Mike had returned from delivering Melvin Klein back to the festival. Virgil had taken Millie and Gabe back to the shelter and went home to rest before coming back to patrol the festival. Dave told Mike that he'd be back later and took Warren out to their cars. They drove to the house and into the drive. Sarah's car was parked and she was leaning against it as Van Gogh ran around the yard.

She grinned seeing Warren as he exited his car and went to her. He gave her a big hug, then said, "You still look beautiful. Get rid of Dave and run off with me."

"Not a chance," she said pushing him back gently. "I like it here and Dave keeps me amused."

"Amused? Is that what I do? Thanks," Dave said as he roughed up Van Gogh.

The dog went over and sniffed Warren, then snorted and moved away.

"Did you get a cat, Warren? Van Gogh smelled something he didn't like," Sarah said.

"I was at my sister's house, she has cats."

"That explains it. Let's go in the house," Dave said. He called Van Gogh and the dog ran to the porch. They went in and over to the living room.

"No new blood stains?" Warren asked.

"Don't start that. I want no more shooting of criminals in this house," Sarah said harshly.

They sat and talked about what they had done since they last saw each other in Las Vegas. Mostly nothing, just small talk. Dave was really wondering what Sarah had to tell him.

"So, do I get the guest room, or are you going to force me to sleep on an air mattress that I have to blow back up every hour?" Warren asked.

"You can have the guest room," Sarah said. "Just don't make a mess."

"Me? Never. Well, you two have some things to talk about and I need my beauty sleep. See you in the morning." He stood and went to the guest room, after picking up his overnight bag by the front door.

Dave sat quietly until Sarah came over to him on the couch. "So, you had something to tell me?" he asked.

"The more I think about it, the sillier it seems. Lois and I went to this fortune teller at the festival and she…well, she gave me a bad reading."

"How so?" Dave asked.

Sarah told him the whole story as he listened. He wasn't happy that this woman had upset his wife and would look into her tomorrow. Fortune telling in the county was banned by ordinance, but they had let it go for the festival as entertainment.

"She was just trying to sound official and shouldn't have touched on such a delicate subject," Dave said. "I'll go have a talk with her tomorrow and straighten her out on what should be entertaining. She's lucky we don't shut her down."

"I don't want to cause trouble. The festival is supposed to be fun, but this woman really did upset me." She kissed Dave on the cheek, then said, "Now, let's change the subject and talk about this boarder you want to share us with."

"Gabe. Yes, Millie said they didn't have any foster care homes to place him right now, maybe in a week or two, but I thought you may like the idea of training with a young boy for when you are a real mother."

"You do know there is a lot of responsibility taking care of an older child. He's probably set in his ways from his home that he suffered through."

"True, but he is a smart kid and I think he just needs some stability for now. You and Van Gogh can whip him into a fine upstanding citizen. He may be in our fair town for a long time if they place him in a foster home here." Dave paused. "He needs to be in a home for Halloween, not in some shelter on a cot with candy from a machine."

"You make it sound so bad. Okay, let's give him a couple days here to see how he does."

"You are such a humanitarian," Dave smiled.

*

Chapter 13

"We're going to pick up Gabe at the shelter," Dave told Warren early the next morning. "I talked to Millie already and she's going to have him ready to go."

"I'll go over to the station and relax until I hear word from Portland. I don't want to bug them, so I'll give them some room," Warren replied.

"I'll be in as soon as I get Sarah and Gabe set up here. I don't think Gabe had any clothes other than the few they had for boys at the shelter. So I'll see if Sarah can take him shopping."

Sarah came out looking refreshed. "I'm ready to pick up Gabe if you are," she said.

Dave and Sarah left Warren to finish his breakfast and drove to the shelter next to the county building. Millie Davis was in her office and greeted them.

"I haven't told Gabe yet, I wanted you to surprise him. This is so good of you to do this," she told Sarah.

"Well, it's sad when anyone is alone in a shelter. Dave said he's a good boy."

"He is, and has been very cooperative and polite since he's been here. I'll take you to him." She led Dave and Sarah to the large room where Gabe sat by himself at a table playing with Lego blocks. He turned his head when they came in and grinned at Dave.

They went to him, and Millie said, "Gabe, you know Sheriff Chandler, and this is his wife, Sarah Chandler."

Sarah sat on a chair by Gabe and said, "How are you doing, Gabe?"

He quietly said, "I'm okay."

"Gabe, my husband and I have talked about it, and we'd like you to come stay with us until they find you a more permanent foster home. It would be for Halloween and I could take you out trick or treating. How would you like that?

Gabe's eyes perked up and he gave her a big smile. "I'd like that," he said a little louder now.

Millie said, "You can take him after you fill out a few papers, just formalities."

Fatal Seance

Dave said, "Sarah, you and Gabe sit and talk. I'll go take care of the paperwork." He went off with Millie, while Sarah sat with Gabe.

"Dave told me a little about you and where you came from. We don't need to talk about your past life in Salem, if you'd rather not. I know it had to have been hard on you."

He nodded his head. "I wasn't happy back there. I had to run away and find a better place."

"Have you ever gone trick or treating?"

"Once, when my mother was sober and off drugs. She dressed me like a hobo and we went around. After we got back she took my candy away and kept it for herself."

"Well, that won't happen here. All the candy you get is yours."

Sarah and Gabe were playing with the Lego blocks when Dave came back. "It's all set, we can take Gabe now," he said.

They thanked Millie and went out to the car. Gabe was thrilled when he saw Dave's Range Rover with the sheriff's logo on the sides and flasher on top. "Can you play the siren?" he asked.

They got in and Dave flipped the siren for a couple seconds, and then shut them off. "Can't use the sirens too long, I don't want to frighten people."

Gabe was smiling from the back seat, as Dave drove out. They arrived back at the house and got out. Sarah and Gabe went to the front door and as she opened it, Van Gogh came rushing out, nearly knocking over Gabe.

"Van Gogh, behave!" she commanded. "Sorry, Gabe, I forgot to warn you about our dog."

Gabe was laughing as he was wrestling with the animal. "I never had a dog before," he said loudly, over Van Gogh's playful growling.

Dave laughed and said, "I think you three will be all right. I need to go into work. Can you take him shopping for some clothes?"

"I can, and it will be fun. I'll need some cash, though," she said.

Dave took out his credit card and gave it to her. "Don't go over the limit," he said, kissed her and turned to Gabe. "I have to go play police, Gabe. Sarah will take you to get some new clothes, so have a good time."

Fatal Seance

He went out to the car and left. Sarah let Van Gogh outside to do his business and she sat with Gabe on the porch.

"It's pretty out here," Gabe said. "I lived in a dirty neighborhood with people who weren't very nice."

"This is the country life for us. It's quiet here and lots of fresh air and squirrels," she said as Van Gogh chased a few. They knew each other and made a grand play out of running around the yard.

Van Gogh finally finished chasing his little friends and came back to the porch and tried to jump up on Gabe. The boy laughed loudly as Sarah pulled the dog away and put him in the house.

"Let's go shopping," she said and they went to Sarah's car.

Dave entered the station to find Warren sitting at his desk. "If you are going to use my desk, you can do my job."

"No problem, you do so little anyway," Warren replied.

Dave came through the swinging half door of the counter to his desk. He said, "Mike, were there any problems at the festival last night?"

"Nothing that Virgil and the deputies couldn't handle. No arrests and only a couple tickets cited. Otherwise a peaceful event so far."

"That's what I like to hear." He turned back to Warren. "I don't suppose you got any word on Rothberg?"

"Nope, still waiting," Warren replied.

"Dave, I almost forgot," Mike said. "There was an email from that carnie guy I took out yesterday. He forgot he took a picture of the van as it was leaving and got the license plate number. I ran it and the plates are registered to Jake Langley of Salem. The van was reported stolen a couple days ago and was found abandoned yesterday by the Salem Police."

"Well, we know that Rothberg is back in Salem. If they can track him down," Warren said. "I'll call the Portland FBI and let them know he's definitely back in town." He pulled out his cell phone and placed the call.

Dave gently pulled Warren out of his chair and sat as Warren moved to the counter.

"Mike, when Virgil gets in, you can go patrol the festival. Just don't spend too much time in the food tent."

Mike laughed and said, "I'm trying to watch my weight now, so I'll avoid the greasy food they serve."

Warren finished his call, came back to Dave and sat on the side chair. "Portland FBI says they got an address from Rothberg's parole officer, but he wasn't at the address. They were told he's been gone for three days. Since before he came up here to get the drugs. They got the local cops involved and it's only matter of time. If he's in the city, they'll find him."

*

Chapter 14

"Are they going to deliver him up here, so we can prosecute him?" Dave asked.

"Hopefully. Do we have all the evidence to do that?" Warren replied.

"We'll get Klein to testify that they took the drugs, we got the video from the motel of Rothberg dropping off the dead body of Doolard and the photo of both of them together in the van. Can you see if they'll dust the van for prints and look for blood after they recover it?"

"I told them about that when I called just now. They'll seize the van and take it in for forensics to examine." Warren said. "We have a good case, but nothing solid saying Rothberg murdered Doolard."

"You'll beat a confession out of him," Dave laughed.

"True, all in the name of justice." Warren replied.

Fatal Seance

The office phone rang and Mike answered, "Sheriff's office, may I help you?" He listened, then called to Dave. "It's Doc Norris, he wants to talk to you."

"Thanks, Mike," Dave said as he lifted his desk phone and pushed a button. "Good morning, Doc. Got something for me on the body?" Dave hit the speaker button so Warren could hear.

"Well, we know he was shot, definitely. From the angle of the shot he was hit from the left side, which makes me believe he was in the passenger seat, shot at close range, about two feet and pushed out the door to the road. If so, there would be blood splatter in the vehicle."

"That's good because they now have the van we believe he was murdered in. We're waiting to hear if there are prints or blood. If they find blood, I'll have them get in touch with you for a type match. Thanks, Doc."

"Glad to help, talk later," he said and hung up.

"I'm seeing this getting tied up tighter for Rothberg. Now if they can find him," Dave said.

Mike cleared his throat, and said, "Dave, you asked me to call Salem Social Services about Gabe."

"Yeah, what did you find out?"

"They said that Gabe was placed in a home and then ran away. I didn't mention he was here, but asked how his foster home managed to let that happen. They said the home is now under investigation for mistreatment of the children. They asked if I knew where he was, I said he's under protection of our CPS agency here and would be staying for now. They said that was good and would need paperwork to transfer his files. I gave her the phone number here and the fax number to send the paperwork. The lady I talked to also warned that the mother may have a problem with him being here if they let her out of rehab."

"I'll talk to Millie Davis and see what we can do to prevent that. Thanks Mike," Dave said. He turned back to Warren and said, "I need to go out to the festival to have a talk with a fortune teller. Want to get your palm read?"

"If it's a nice shade of red, I might."

"Mike, I'll be out at the festival. Call if something comes up." He stood and the men went out to the cruiser.

"Not using your Rover?" Warren asked.

Fatal Seance

"No, I'm trying to keep the mileage down," he said and they pulled out. Dave explained what was bothering Sarah as they drove.

"That's not exactly entertaining. We get a number of complaints about mediums, psychics and other con games. Hard to keep up with them if people don't complain."

They parked by the Olympia deputies' cars and went in the festival. Dave and Warren headed to the area for the sideshow and found the tent of the fortune teller. There were a few people waiting to get in, but Dave went to the head of the line and told the next customers to wait. They went in and found the woman was just finishing up with her current customers. Dave stood waiting until the people left and the woman stared at them.

Dave went closer and could see she was around thirty and fairly attractive.

"May I help you, officer?" she asked.

"It's Sheriff. Where is the older woman who was here yesterday?"

"Older woman? There is no older woman working this attraction. I'm the only one who runs this sideshow."

"My wife and her friend were here yesterday and had an older woman in her late seventies, from what I'm told, gave them a reading with tarot cards."

"Sheriff, we don't use tarot cards, they take too long to read, so I just read palms and the crystal ball. It's all for entertainment, of course. There was no older woman working here."

"Do you work all day or take a break to eat?"

"I do take a lunch, yes."

"What time did you take a lunch yesterday?"

She thought for a moment, "Sometime between two and three, and I ate in the employee food tent."

Dave pulled his cell phone and speed dialed Sarah. She came on and Dave asked her what time she saw the fortune teller. Sarah told him that she and Lois went there around two-thirty. He thanked her and hung up.

"How long did you eat?"

"About an hour, I was tired and not rushing to get back to the tent."

"Well, while you were out, someone came in and pretended to be the fortune teller. Why?"

"I have no idea. I would never permit it. I have to be careful, as you know fortune telling is illegal in some areas. Except for entertainment as I do here."

Dave didn't know what to say. He looked at Warren and said, "Let's go." He turned back to the woman, "Sorry to have bothered you. Just remember you are only doing this for entertainment, don't upset any people, or I'll close you down."

"I'll remember that Sheriff, thank you."

Dave and Warren went out and stood looking around. "Something is wrong here. Sarah and Lois couldn't have been mistaken about what happened. I may have to do some more checking on this fortune teller."

Warren's cell phone buzzed and he answered, listened, then hung up. "Interesting. Portland FBI said they got a call about Rothberg breaking some woman out of the rehab center there in Salem. They said the woman's name was Abby Doolard. Could that be Gabe's mother?"

"I never asked her first name. How did they know it was Rothberg who freed her?"

"Well, the dummy signed in under his own name to talk with her. After they found her gone they called the local cops who already had an FBI BOLO out for Rothberg. They called the FBI and they called me. Now we have two fugitives on the run."

"I wonder where they would go." Dave said.

Dave's cell phone buzzed, he saw it was Mike. "Yeah, Mike," he answered and put the phone on speaker.

"Dave, I just got a call from the child protective people in Salem, using the number I gave them. They said that Gabe's mother came in with some man and forced one of the workers to tell her where Gabe was. The worker said she couldn't tell them, so they shot her in the leg. She finally gave them the town's name, Brinnon, Washington. The mother shot the social worker and they left."

*

Chapter 15

"Damn," Dave uttered. "Thanks, Mike. If you hear anything more, call." He hung up and said to Warren, "I have a feeling they're on their way here. Why is the mother so hot to get her son back?"

"Does Gabe have some information that she wants?" Warren asked.

"I don't know. But we have to be on the lookout for them. Let's get back to the office."

They left the festival and drove back to the station.

"I'll call the Seattle FBI SAIC and let him know what is going on. Maybe he can put out a BOLO to watch for them. There's only one main road leading up here from Portland. We could put cars on the highway to stop them."

"We have to do something. I'm worried for Gabe, if his mother is hell-bent enough to shoot a government employee to get the location of her son. I'll have to warn Sarah, too," Dave said.

"Does Sarah still have her own gun?" Warren asked.

"She does, I may have her start carrying it. Just to be cautious."

They arrived back and went inside. "Mike, any more news?"

"Nothing here. I called the Salem police and talked to them about the shooting at the CPS office. The detective I talked to has warrants out for them. I told him the FBI is already searching. Since it was a state employee shot, they are going to watch but let the FBI take lead."

"Thanks, Mike, very good follow up," Warren said. Mike smiled at the compliment.

"I'll call the state police and have them put road blocks on the 101 into town. We may be jumping the gun, but better to be safe than sorry. They both have murdered now, so they both are dangerous." Dave went to his desk and placed a call. Warren was standing at the counter when the front door opened and he was surprised to see who came in.

"Walt! You made it," Warren said happily.

"I finished up with the surveillance and made my reports. The terrorist cell has been shut down," Walt replied.

"You do your country proud," Warren shook Walt's hand and said, "I hope you're finished with things that Homeland Security should be doing."

"I'm all yours now."

Dave finished his call to the State Police and came to the counter. "Walt, good to see you. You're just in time for some action. We have two possible killers heading our way."

"That's better than sitting in my van all day watching people come and go. I need some action," Walt said.

"I'll let Warren fill you in on the details," he said to Walt, then said to Warren, "I had Mike send the rap sheet on Rothberg to the State Police so they know who to look for. I also asked him to see if the mother has priors, besides drugs. It would be good to have a picture of her."

"Now you have to warn Sarah, just to get her ready," Warren said.

"Yeah, she would appreciate knowing that," Dave said. "She should still be out shopping so I'll wait until we go to the house. It's a little less than 230 miles to Salem, so it would take almost four hours to drive."

"If they're driving carefully, so not to attract attention," Warren added.

"They'd probably stop for food, so I figure they wouldn't get up here until later. Enough time for the State Police to set up road blocks."

"We need to catch them, so wouldn't the road blocks scare them away?" Warren asked.

"Good point. We don't know why Abby Doolard wants her son so badly that she'd murder for him. I'd say they'll make an effort to get up here. If they see the road block, they'll find another way around."

"So, you think we should let them get up here and take them out ourselves?" Warren asked.

"I'd hate to take the chance that we'd screw up and get someone killed," Dave replied.

"Us? Screw up? Never. We've taken down a good number of killers and generally bad men, we can take down one man and one woman," Warren boasted.

Fatal Seance

Dave grinned and turned to Mike. "We need to keep an eye on the festival and the killers. Call Olympia and see if we can get a couple more deputies. This is going to be a manhunt, and a womanhunt, too." Mike nodded and picked up his phone.

"Speaking of the festival, what about Klein?" Warren asked. "He fingered Rothberg and I'm sure Rothberg knows Klein can identify him. He's our only witness. Shouldn't we protect Klein?"

"Another good point. Boy, you're on a roll today. I'll have Virgil watch Klein. That should keep him busy."

On cue, the front door opened and in came Virgil. "Hey Walt, good to see you," he said. Walt acknowledged him.

"Virgil, I need you to go to the festival and keep an eye on Klein, the carnie from yesterday. We think Rothberg is heading this way and since Klein is our witness, we need to keep him alive. Do what you have to, even arrest him into protective custody if needed."

"Sure Dave, I'll go right now," he said and went back out.

Bob Moats

Dave turned to Mike and said, "When the deputies from Olympia get here, have one of them watch the office, show him the ropes and take the rest out to the festival to relieve the others. Then you go get some sleep and come back in here to man the office in a couple hours. Until Rothberg and Doolard are captured, we all have to run doubles."

Dave turned to Warren and said, "I think we should go warn Sarah and see what Gabe can tell us about his mother. It may help to catch her."

They went out to their cars, Walt had his fancy black van with all the electronic gear that he was so proud of. It was a rolling spy vehicle and high tech office.

"Good to see the supervan again," Warren said with a grin.

Walt smiled and they went to their vehicles and drove out. They arrived back at the house, just as Sarah and Gabe were unloading packages.

"Walt, you're back," Sarah said with a smile as the men approached. Walt smiled back as Dave went to Sarah. Dave told Gabe to go let Van Gogh out of the house. The boy ran off after Sarah gave him the door key.

Fatal Seance

"I have some news that you need to hear. It seems our killer, Rothberg, broke Gabe's mother out of rehab and then she shot and killed a social worker in Salem. She was looking for Gabe, and got the information that he was up here," he paused to let that sink in.

"So, she's coming here?" Sarah asked.

"It looks that way. I'd like you to start carrying your gun again."

"Damn straight I will. If she even steps foot on this property, she'll regret it."

"Try not to shoot her in the house, if you can," Dave said with a grin. "We don't need any more blood on the carpet."

Gabe was running around with the dog as Dave called him over. He came up and gave Sarah the keys back.

Dave took everyone to the porch and had Gabe sit. "I have to ask you something Gabe. What was your mother's first name?"

The boy got a puzzled look and said, "Abigail. They called her Abby for short. Why?"

*

Chapter 16

Dave sat next to the boy on the porch and paused. "Gabe, your mother may be coming here to get you."

The boy looked panicked. "No, stop her. I don't want to see her."

"Calm down, Gabe. We won't let her get near you. She's a wanted criminal now. I have to ask something. You told me before that your mother didn't care about you, so do you know why she wants you back now?"

The boy was silent for a while, everyone waited. Sarah sat on the other side of him. "Gabe, they need to know what to expect and why your mother is coming here. If you have something to say that would help, please tell us. We won't hurt you if you did something wrong."

Gabe looked at Sarah, "I didn't do anything wrong. My mother wants me because of the money I have coming."

"What money?" Dave asked.

Fatal Seance

"The money my grandfather left me when he died. My grandpa was my dad's father. He didn't like my dad because he was a bad man and in prison, so he left all his money to me in his will. It was put in something about a bank," he paused, thinking.

"Was it a trust?" Sarah asked.

"Yeah, that's it, a trust. They said I could get the money when I turned sixteen. My dad couldn't touch the money, and my uncle tried to get hold of me to take the money."

"Do you know how much money is in your trust?" Warren asked.

Gabe looked at him and said, "I was told it was twenty billion dollars."

"Do you mean twenty million dollars?" Dave asked.

The boy looked confused and thought about it. "Yeah, you're right, it was twenty million dollars and a lot of property somewhere in Oregon, with lots of trees."

"Was your grandfather in the lumber business?" Dave asked.

"I think he was. I remember hearing him talking about the quality of lumber."

"So, your mother takes you and keeps you until you can get the money. Then she'll take it from you. Is that the idea?"

"I guess so. She doesn't want me otherwise," he said sadly.

Dave looked at Sarah, "Take Gabe in the house to try on his new clothes."

She agreed and she took him in the house, followed by Van Gogh.

Dave stood and took Warren and Walt aside and said, "I understand why she wants Gabe now. She has the money in mind. She and Rothberg must be working together in this. Rothberg murders the uncle to take him out of the picture of getting any money. The father is in prison and can't touch the money. The mother was left out of the will, so the only way she could grab the money is to wait until Gabe gets the money and she'll do away with him. As his mother, it all goes to her as the only heir."

"Dave, the boy is twelve," Warren said. "There's still four years before he can collect, so she'll have to be sure he doesn't get hurt until after he collects."

"I feel sorry for the boy," Dave said. "He'll never know who really cares for him. They'll only want his money."

"Yeah, he's got a rough ride ahead," Warren said.

Dave's cell phone buzzed, he looked, it was Mike. "Yeah, Mike, what now?" He put it on speaker.

"Dave, I got a call from Olympia sheriffs. They set up their own road block below the city and said they spotted Rothberg according to this mug shot."

"Did they stop them?" Dave asked.

"No, they managed to get through, but they aren't heading here, they went out Interstate five towards Tacoma. Possibly heading towards Seattle. I called Tacoma PD and warned them, but they already had a call from the sheriffs in Olympia. That's all they've got for now, but they'll be watching."

"Thanks Mike, keep me informed." He hung up. "Well, we may have a reprieve for now. If they are going into Tacoma or up to Seattle, it will be a while before they get back here."

"Why would they be going that way if they want the boy?" Walt asked.

"Good question. Maybe it has to do with the drugs Rothberg took from Klein. Maybe they're going to sell them in the city. Then come here for Gabe."

"Whatever, the network is hot to find them. We got city police, state police and FBI all on the lookout. They're celebrities now."

Sarah came to the door and called to them. "Come on in and see what costume Gabe is going to wear for Halloween."

The men went in the house and she took them to the living room. Gabe was standing in the middle of the room as Van Gogh sat next to him. Dave laughed out loud.

The boy had on a sheriff's costume, complete with a sidearm. Dave went to the boy and studied the costume. Gabe was beaming with joy.

"You used my old uniform, with all the patches," he said. "I like the holster and gun, did you buy it today?"

"There was a Halloween costume shop so I got the shirt and moved a couple of your old patches to it," Sarah said.

Dave grinned and went to a closet. He went in and came out with a baseball cap. It had a sheriff's badge patch on the front. He took it to Gabe and adjusted the cap, placing it on his head.

"That's better. Now you look official. Just don't arrest anyone for now."

"Can I arrest my mother?" Gabe asked.

Dave was surprised by his statement. "Leave that up to the adult police, Gabe. You can watch."

"Is my mother still coming?" he asked.

"Well, at last report, she and her friend were heading towards Seattle. So they won't be back for a while. You can relax and have a good Halloween." Dave said and turned to Sarah. "Where are you going to take him?"

"I figured through that new subdivision. It should be good pickings."

"Great, I'm going to have Mike escort the two of you around."

"One little sheriff and one over-weight sheriff," Sarah laughed.

"Don't say that out loud to Mike. He's trying to lose some weight."

"I'll be discreet," she laughed.

~~*~~

"Damn it, Abby. They're on our trail," Rothberg yelled at the closed door of the bathroom in the motel they stopped at to lay low for a while.

"Well, if you hadn't signed in with your real name at rehab, they wouldn't have known you," she yelled back out. The door opened and she came out. "Dumb move, jackass."

"Don't call me that, bitch. They asked for my ID, what was I supposed to do?"

"Whatever, we just keep moving and stay ahead of them," she replied.

"I don't see how you're going to pull this off. If you get the kid back, what are you going to do? The cops will be after your ass to bring you down."

"After we sell the drugs in Seattle through my contact, we'll have the cash to go to a non-extradition country. After the time passes, as his mother, I can collect on behalf of Gabe and have the money transferred to our bank. Then we kill the kid."

*

Chapter 17

The next twenty-four hours were quiet, Rothberg and Doolard had gone off the grid. Police were still watching, but were pulling back now. Warren and Walt had spent the down time relaxing and fishing. Sarah and Gabe were spending time together getting used to each other. The festival was half done and Dave was now concerned about the fortune teller.

Sarah came in the station with Gabe to show the boy what the inside of the sheriff's office was like. "Mike, take our young man and show him to the lock-up," Dave said to his deputy.

Mike grinned and took Gabe to the cells. Dave turned to Sarah, "I need you to think about your visit to the fortune teller. You said she was an old lady, in her eighties or so, right?"

"She was, you can even ask Lois. I don't understand what you told me yesterday about her not being there. I thought about it and I know I wasn't dreaming."

"I think we need to gather Lois and take a trip to the carnival and talk to someone in charge," Dave said.

"I'll call her and have her meet us. Do you want to do this now?"

"May as well. It's been fairly quiet around here. May as well take care of it before the carnival pulls out tomorrow night."

Sarah took out her phone and called Lois. She sat on a bench across from the counter and explained to Lois the events of Dave going to the fortune teller's tent. Lois told her she could come to the house and they finished the call. Sarah went back to Dave.

119

Fatal Seance

Sarah told Dave about the call as Mike was bringing Gabe out from the back.

"I showed him the cells and the interrogation room. He likes our break room," Mike told Dave and Sarah.

Gabe was grinning from ear to ear and said, "I'd like to be a sheriff one day."

"It's a lot of long hours and can be dangerous," Dave warned. "You have to study hard in school and then go through police training. It's not a job you can just be hired in."

Gabe agreed, "I'll let you tell me what to do."

"Gabe, you have at least nine years before you can apply to be a sheriff. Take your time, you may want to do something else later." Dave thought about the money the boy would inherit and figured he'd change his mind about being a cop. "So, Gabe, do you feel like going back out to the carnival?"

The boy looked excited and said so. "I'd like that just fine, sheriff."

Dave told Mike he was going to be gone for a while and took Sarah and Gabe back to the house, to see what Warren and Walt were up to and wait for Lois.

At the house, Sarah went to get Gabe's new jacket, since it was starting to get cold out. Two days until Halloween and fall was coming on strong.

Dave went to the back door looking out to the Hood Canal, and saw Warren and Walt in his boat. "Hey," he yelled. "We're going to the carnival to visit a fortune teller, want to come?"

Warren said something to Walt then yelled back, "Thanks, we're good here."

"Okay, I'll leave this door unlocked. Watch the dog." Dave went back in and heard a car in the drive. It was Lois.

Dave, Sarah and Gabe went out to greet Lois. "I don't understand who that old woman was. Do you think the young woman lied to you, Dave?"

"I'm wondering that. I just want to ask a few more questions. You two are my witnesses."

They all got in Dave's Rover and he drove out.

On the way, Sarah introduced Gabe to Lois. "How are you?" Lois asked.

"I'm fine, ma'am," he replied.

"So polite," she said. "Is Gabe staying with you now?" she asked Sarah.

"Until they can find him a decent foster home. We're going to have a nice Halloween trick or treating. What are you going to do, Lois?"

"There's a Halloween party at the VFW, I'm trying to decide if I want to go. Where are you going to hit houses?"

"That new subdivision. Gabe should get a bag full of candy," she said and smiled at the boy.

Dave pulled into the festival grounds and parked next to the Olympia Deputies' cars. They went into the midway and Dave said he wanted to check on Virgil, still watching Klein. They went to the tilt-a-whirl and found Virgil standing on the side watching the crowd. He waved to Dave and came up.

"Are you bored yet?" Dave asked him.

"No, this isn't bad. I get to see all the beautiful women screaming on the ride," he said with a grin.

"Rothberg still hasn't been sighted. FBI thinks he's in Seattle and they're watching for him. Did you get a copy of the woman's photo that Mike got?"

"I got both photos, so I know who I'm looking for. Klein has been real cooperative. He says he's not interested in dying. So he doesn't mind me following him around."

"I'll have a relief for you with a deputy from Olympia. So hang in here. We're going to see a fortune teller."

They left Virgil to his watch and went to the tent of the fortune teller. There were no customers at the opening so Dave entered. He had Sarah, Lois and Gabe hold back behind him. The same young woman was sitting at the table.

"Well, sheriff, back to get your fortune this time?" she asked.

"No, I want some answers," he pointed to Sarah and Lois, and said, "I brought my wife and her friend, who were in here the other day. They both saw a woman in her eighties who gave them a reading with tarot cards."

"As I said, sheriff, I don't use tarot cards. It takes too long to give a reading, and there is no other person working this sideshow, other than me."

Fatal Seance

Sarah moved forward and said, "I hate to call you a liar, but I had an old woman tell me I was going to have a terrible thing happen to me. That's not what I expect from what is supposed to be entertainment. She charged us ten dollars each and gave us nothing of value."

"I don't charge more than two dollars for a palm reading or crystal gazing. I'm not calling you a liar, but there has been no one else in this tent other than me."

"The time my wife was here was the same time you took a lunch, or so you said. Could someone have slipped in and gave readings to people?"

"I won't say it couldn't have happened. I don't know anyone traveling with this carnival that even fits your description of the old woman. The oldest woman traveling with us is in her fifties and good looking."

Dave looked at Sarah and she shrugged. "I don't know what to say. We saw her and she gave us a reading."

Dave turned back to the woman, "Okay, we have no proof, so you better watch your tent better when you take a lunch break. I don't want to hear any more complaints about this mystery woman."

"I'll be more careful, sheriff, thank you."

Dave took the women and boy out and down the midway. In the small tent, a back flap opened and an old woman called in. "Are they gone?"

*

Chapter 18

"Mother, I lied to that cop, and I told you to stay out of the tent."

"Angela, I knew that woman was going to be here. I had to warn her."

"Stop with your psychic predictions, will you? You haven't been right yet. Now go hide until we leave this town. I don't want to get shut down or arrested for lying to the law."

The woman frowned. "That woman needed to be warned."

"You already did that, and frightened her. Bad enough she's the sheriff's wife. Now go and stay in the trailer."

The woman closed the flap and went off. The young woman turned just as two young girls came in. "Welcome, come in, sit and I'll read your fortune."

~~*~~

Gabe was enjoying the rides with Sarah. Lois said she wasn't feeling up to going on the rides. Dave left them to wander the midway so he could check on the deputies. He was satisfied they were doing their jobs and found Sarah watching Gabe on a merry-go-round horse. Lois was on the bench seat of the ride, smiling.

"I think Lois is going through another childhood. Gabe is enjoying himself. Any word on his mother?" Sarah asked.

"None. It's like they just disappeared. I'm worried that they may show up anytime. Do you have your gun?"

Sarah subtlety pulled back her jacket showing the .38 in its holster.

"Good girl, now don't shoot the wrong people."

"Hey, I'm a good shot, and I know who the wrong people are who need to be shot. I saw the photos of Rothberg and Abby that Virgil had, so I know them now."

"Good, let's gather our children and head out. I have to change the deputies before they wear down. I've got more replacements coming."

The ride ended and Lois got off, followed by Gabe. "Did you have a good day?" Dave asked Gabe.

"I did, thank you," he replied.

They went back to the car and drove to the house.

"I have to get back to selling houses. Thank you for the fun, Dave," Lois said and went to her car. Sarah took Gabe into the house to get something to eat.

Warren came out of the house and over to Dave. "So, did you settle with the gypsy?"

"Got nothing but talk. There's not much I can do. Sarah had her feelings hurt, but that's not a crime. We'll just write it off for now."

"Well, if it's any consolation, I got a call from Seattle and they had a sighting of Rothberg and his moll on a surveillance camera at a bank. Seems they went in to get their money changed, they had lots of hundred dollar bills. That's a signal to most big city banks that the money could be drug money. Drug dealers like to use big bills to sell and buy drugs, easier to carry a bunch of one hundred dollar bills than twenties."

"I can see that. Did they get their change?"

"Nope, the cashier was acting suspicious and that must have given Rothberg a warning, so they scooted out before the cops could arrive. They reviewed the surveillance videos and recognized who they were. At least we know now that they sold their drugs and have cash."

"And it's a matter of time before they head back here for Gabe," Dave said.

"I think they'll lay low again. They were identified on the video, so their traveling will wait until the heat dies down."

"The two of them aren't very bright are they? They pretty much didn't think this out very well," Dave said.

"No, Abby is now a wanted murderer, and she'll never be able to take possession of Gabe, legally or otherwise. They have her on video shooting the social worker, so it's pretty much a good to go for conviction."

"What if she kidnaps him?" Dave asked.

"And do what? She'd have to leave the country or keep on the run for four years."

"For twenty million reasons she could hide out that long," Dave said. "I'd say she'd leave the country. Then wait it out, find a shyster lawyer when Gabe is old enough. All they have to do is give him his inheritance and then she could do away with the boy through an accident. As his mother, she could get the money."

"She'd have to live in some jungle to enjoy the money, she couldn't come back here."

"And I'm sure if the father gets out of prison, he'd make Abby's life a living hell. Maybe you should see if you can get him paroled," Dave said with a laugh.

"I can't condone murder. But in some cases, I don't know," Warren said.

"Well, she needs to be stopped," Dave said as Sarah came back out to them carrying a sandwich.

"Is that for me?" Dave asked.

Sarah took a bite and said, "I made this for me. Get your own."

"I love you, too," Dave replied as his cell phone buzzed. He pulled it out and saw it was Virgil.

"What's up, Virg?" Dave answered and put the phone on speaker.

"My relief came to watch Klein, I'm back at the station and a call came in about Rothberg."

"Okay, what was it?" Dave asked when Virgil didn't continue.

"They caught him on video shooting a convenience store employee in Redmond, Washington."

"Redmond? That's northeast of Seattle, why are they up there?" Warren asked.

"They're probably going over to route 203 which goes around Seattle," Walt said. "They may be trying to avoid going close to Seattle."

"That's a long way to go, Walt. It'll take them a couple days going that way," Warren replied.

"They have time to kill. Gabe doesn't inherit for four years, so why rush?" Dave added. "Thanks, Virgil, keep me informed." He hung up the phone.

"I'm wondering if they'll just keep tabs on Gabe now and wait until he is old enough to inherit," Warren said.

"But if they have him, they'd have better control as to the money. They could use him for ransom," Dave said.

"This is making my head hurt, I'm going in to clean the fish we caught and make a great dinner for everyone," Warren said.

"You're going to make dinner?" Sarah asked him.

"I can cook. Just watch me." He turned and went to the house.

"He is a good cook," Walt said and followed him.

131

Fatal Seance

An hour later they all sat around the dinner table and enjoyed Warren's fish dinner.

"You amaze me, Warren," Dave said. "I didn't know you could cook."

"One of my little secrets," he beamed.

There was a knock on the front door and everyone jumped. Dave had his hand on his weapon as he went to the door. He looked out the side window and saw an old woman, dressed in the garb of a person reminding him of a gypsy. Warren was standing behind him as Dave opened the door.

"May I help you?" he asked.

"I need to see the woman of the house," she said with a thick Slavic accent.

"Why?" Dave replied.

"It's important she knows the rest of what I couldn't finish the other day."

"You were in the fortune teller's tent," Dave said.

"I was, but she rushed out before I could finish. It's important I speak to her."

*

Chapter 19

Sarah was standing behind Warren and came around both of the men. "You were the one who gave me that bad reading," she said.

"It was only bad because you left before I finished. I needed to complete the reading."

Sarah looked at Dave and nodded. "Let her in and hear her out," she said.

Warren stepped back as Dave opened the screen door, allowing the woman to enter.

"How did you find us?" Dave asked.

"I know many things. I have psychic powers, which many scoff at."

Fatal Seance

Dave looked out to the driveway, there was no car. "How did you get here?"

"I walked," she said, like it was no big feat.

Dave knew it was eight miles to the festival grounds, but said nothing. He led her to the living room. Sarah was keeping her distance from the old woman.

"Sit here," Dave said, pointing to a chair. "Now, what do you have to tell us?"

"I have to speak with the woman, she is the person who needs to know."

"How do you know me?" Sarah asked moving towards the woman.

"I saw you in a vision. You will be very brave and help people. But you will lose a child."

Dave started to say something, but Sarah stopped him. "What child? Speak quickly or I'll have my husband throw you out."

"I saw you in my vision, coming to the carnival, and to the tent. I had to speak to you."

"And you did, now what child?"

"The boy in your care. He is in great danger and will be taken. You will lose him."

Sarah stiffened and looked back at Gabe still by the dining table. "Explain your meaning, quickly," she spoke harshly.

"I saw bad evil coming for him. People who are not good, who want something from him."

"How could she know this?" Warren said quietly to Dave.

"What will happen?" Dave asked the woman.

"People will attempt to take the boy away, far away. You must stop them."

"How?" Warren asked.

"I can't tell you, my vision ended. But you must be aware of the danger. The child will save himself and one close to him. That's all I can say." She stood and went to the front door. She turned, saying, "Thank you for giving me the time." She went out the door.

Everyone stood motionless, stunned by what just happened. Dave went to the door and looked out. The woman was gone. He called to Warren and they both went out to find the woman, but the yard was empty.

"How did she get away so quickly?" Warren asked.

"I don't know, but this is getting spooky," Dave replied.

"There's no way the woman could have known about Rothberg and Doolard, or Gabe," Warren said.

"I'll be glad when the carnival leaves town, along with Rothberg and Doolard being captured," Dave said.

"Or killed," Warren added.

"That, too. I need to see how Sarah is taking this." He turned and went back in.

Sarah was holding on to Gabe, very motherly like. "I'll be damned if anyone takes this boy," she said firmly.

"We'll all be on alert," Dave assured her.

"Is she walking back to the carnival?" Sarah asked.

"I don't know, she disappeared. She's nowhere to be seen."

Sarah was speechless. She looked shocked. Then, "I don't know who that woman was, but she was too close to the truth for me."

"Unfortunately, she didn't give us any word on finding Rothberg or Abby. That would have been more helpful than a warning," Warren said.

~~*~~

"Why the hell did we go this way? It's all woods and no civilization. I need a drink, do you think there's a bar around here?" Rothberg groaned.

"Shut up and drive. We can't go on the roads through Seattle and Tacoma. They have the roads being watched now," Abby said. "We have to be extra careful now. You shouldn't have shot that guy in the store."

"He acted like he knew me."

"Yeah, and you're on the video now. If I hadn't seen that cop car coming up the road, I would have gone in the back and pulled the tapes."

"Maybe we'll make the news. Let's find a motel to crash and see what the news has. I've never been on TV before."

"You dumb bastard, if they run your picture, everyone will know you. How far do you think we'll get if they know what you look like."

Rothberg didn't answer. He drove quietly for another five miles until they came to a roadside motel and diner.

"You stay in the car," Abby said. "I'll go get a room." She got out and went in.

There was an older woman behind the safety glass of the counter. Abby thought it was strange to have the protective glass in such a dive of a motel.

"May I help you?" the woman asked.

"Room for two for the night, please. What's with the glass?" she said pointing.

"Extra protection. We get a lot of undesirables driving this way to avoid going through the cities. We've had trouble before. Got lots of protection

138

now." She pointed to a wall of heavy firepower weapons.

Abby knew this woman meant business, so she didn't challenge her. She signed the book and got the key to the room.

"Check out is eleven. No food in the diner, closed down when the cook was shot by some of those undesirables. You and your friend keep the peace and we'll get along just fine."

"Is there a bar nearby?"

"Five miles down the road, but be careful, it's a biker hangout."

"Okay, do you have a liquor store around?"

"Across the street from the biker bar." The woman gave her a toothy grin.

Abby smiled and left the office. She told Rothberg to get out and go in the room, handing him the key. She stood looking around the area. Secluded and quiet. Other than the roar of a couple motorcycles coming up the road, passing her.

They must have seen her standing there, they spun around and came back, pulling up to her.

Fatal Seance

"Hey sweets, what are you doing out here? Got a room for you and me?" he growled.

"I got dick for you, bitch," she replied.

The biker looked annoyed and dropped his kickstand. He got off and walked to her. He got about ten feet when she pulled out the big .45 from behind her and pointed at his crotch.

"I didn't say who's dick did I? Maybe you'd like to donate?"

The man looked shocked and backed up a little. "Hey, sweets. I just want a little fun, that's all."

"Go find fun elsewhere," she said.

The biker looked to the motel door that just opened and in the doorway stood Rothberg with his gun pointed at the men.

"Okay, I see you have your own fun, Sorry to disturb you." He turned and got on his bike, started it up and drove off, followed by his partner.

She looked back and said, "I need a drink."

*

Chapter 20

Devil's Night.

Dave had watched the carnival close down the rides and pack everything away. He walked through the now folding midway and found that the fortune telling tent was gone.

"Excuse me," he stopped one of the workers pulling down the big sideshow tent. "Do you know where the fortune teller went?"

"She pulled out about an hour ago. You just missed her." He walked away to pack the poles of the tent.

Dave turned to watch the implosion of the rides and the sideshow tent. It was amazing how they pulled everything down, packed and moved on in a matter of hours. He had hoped to talk to the fortune teller about the older woman, but he didn't get back to the festival until late.

He saw Mike standing by Klein and went to him. "Mr. Klein, I'm sorry but I can't let you leave the county. You're a material witness in a drug exchange and murder. We need you here to help convict our killers. You can voluntarily stay with us, or I can arrest you and put you in protective custody. You decide, a nice motel room or a jail cell?"

Klein smiled and said, "Motel room, please."

"Very good. Fortunately, you'll have round the clock protection. You'll not be alone until we find the fugitives and convict them. I'll call the U.S Marshals and have them come in to help watch you."

"Are they going to put me in witness protection?" he asked.

"I highly doubt it for just two criminals you're fingering. A mob or a gang leader, maybe, but not for Rothberg or Doolard."

He looked disappointed, but went along when Mike led him out. He had explained to the carnival bosses about his not going with them and they understood.

Dave turned to Warren coming up from the other end of the grounds. "They're quick to get out, aren't they?" Warren asked.

"They have to go set up in another place and do this all over again. I don't envy them," Dave said.

"This life would be too much for me," Warren said.

Walt came up from another side to the teardown. "It's amazing that they can pack this so quickly."

They stood there watching the last of the rides being hauled away. There were only a couple small trucks doing last minute work of unhooking the power lines. The area went dark in the night, no moon to provide a little light.

"Well, I think we're done here. Let's go back," Dave said.

They got in Dave's Rover and he went back to the house. They drove in and found Lois' car in the drive. "It's kind of late for Lois to visit," Dave said.

"It's only nine-thirty. Not that late for a Friday night," Warren said.

They went in and found Sarah, Gabe and Lois in the living room sitting at a card table. There were four white candles burning around the room and the lights were on low. Sarah turned and smiled at Dave. "Come see what Lois brought us," she said.

The men went to the women and boy, and Dave saw what was on the table, a large Ouija board. "It's an old board that I've had for years," Lois said. "I thought it would be fun to try on Devil's Night."

"So, are you having a séance now?" Dave asked.

"Well, I guess you could say it's like a séance. You don't exactly have a séance with a Ouija board, close, but séances are different. The board only reveals hidden facts through spirits," Lois answered.

"Like where our criminals are?" Warren asked.

"We could ask it, maybe it knows," Sarah said hopefully. "It would be nice to have an idea where they are. Pull up a folding chair and sit in."

Gabe moved away and gave his chair to Dave. He thanked the boy. Warren moved a chair over as Walt stood back.

"Aren't you going to sit in, Walt?" Warren asked his partner.

"No, thank you. Ouija boards are evil, one shouldn't play with them lightly."

Dave looked at him and said, "I had one when I was a boy, we played with it a lot. It didn't possess our souls."

"I've heard stories," Walt replied. "I don't mess with the spirit world."

"For a geek, you believe in spirits?" Warren asked. "I thought you were more analytical than that."

"I am, I just don't fool with some things," Walt said.

"Well, hang on to your gun in case any of us are grabbed by a demon," Warren said trying not to laugh at his partner. "So where do we begin?" Warren asked.

Lois explained the procedure and had everyone put their finger tips on the Planchette, the pointer, and exclaimed loudly, "Spirit, this is a safe place. We only wish to communicate with you, ask you questions and to learn from you. Please come through and talk with us."

Fatal Seance

Warren was trying not to laugh at the seriousness of Lois. Sarah was looking upset and Dave wondered what was wrong.

"Sarah, are you all right?" Dave asked her quietly.

"I just felt a heaviness and a chill. I'll be alright. Lois, continue."

Lois told everyone to just relax and let the planchette do the work. "Does anyone have a question?" Lois asked.

"Where's my mother?" Gabe said quietly, startling everyone.

"Okay, everyone concentrate on that question then. Spirit tell us, where is Abby Doolard?"

They sat watching the pointer, just sitting. "Maybe it's broken," Warren said, just as the pointer started to move. "Whoa," he said quietly.

The pointer moved around the board and stopped over various letters. Dave was calling out the letters. "N…o…r…t…h. North, well, we all knew that." He watched as it moved more. "C…o…m…i…n…g…s…o…o…n. Coming soon. Something else we knew. M…o…n…d…a…y, Monday? Well, we didn't know that."

"You're pushing the thing, Dave," Warren accused him.

"I am not. I'm barely touching it," he defended.

"B…e…w…a…r…e…d…a…n…g…e…r. Okay, now that's a warning if I ever saw one," Dave said. He continued to read the letters. "D…e…a…t…h. But who?"

The pointer moved around selecting letters that spelled, 'a mother', which upset Sarah.

"Let's stop this, it's not fun anymore," Sarah said, thinking of her unborn baby. She was becoming a mother.

"Everyone, move the planchette to the words 'good bye' at the bottom." Lois said, and they forced the pointer to the words. Lois spoke loudly, "Good bye, spirit," and took her hands off the pointer. Everyone else pulled their hands back quickly.

They sat staring at the pointer, as if it would move on its own.

"Boo!" yelled Walt.

Fatal Seance

Everyone jumped and glared at Walt. "Sorry, I couldn't resist," he said, laughing.

"You can sleep in your van tonight. And I hope the spirits invade you," Warren growled.

"I think we've had enough of the Ouija board," Lois said. "It was interesting, to say the least."

"Well, we have an idea when Rothberg and Abby may show up," Warren said.

Sarah sat quietly, then got up and went to the kitchen. Dave followed her as Lois was putting the board away.

"What's the matter?" Dave asked her.

"I've been upset twice this week. First when that gypsy woman said I would lose a child and now the comment on the death of a mother. I'm going to be a mother soon, now I feel scared."

*

Chapter 21

"Sarah, it's just a game. Everyone was moving the thing subconsciously knowing what to say," Dave said trying to reassure Sarah.

"Why did it say that a mother would die?"

"Who knows? When I had my Ouija board, we would get all kinds of dumb things spelled out. None of it was true. Try to take it in the spirit of fun, not bad spirits."

"Dave, I felt something once Lois called the spirit. I felt a heavy presence in the room. I felt a chill go through me, what was that?"

"You were psyched up for the board. That's all. I know you're a strong woman, this isn't like you."

"Dave, my body is changing. This baby is going to mess with my hormones, so expect a lot of changes in me."

He put his arms around her and pulled her close. "I'll do whatever you say, as long as it's reasonable."

Warren came in the kitchen and stopped. "Am I interrupting?"

"No, we were just discussing life," Dave replied. "What's up?"

"I just got a call, Rothberg and Doolard were in a motel on the 203 and there was an altercation with a couple of bikers. Seems Doolard pissed off one of them earlier and they came back to the motel later. There was gunfire and two bikers are dead. Rothberg and Doolard escaped and they're in the wind."

"So they're on the move again. Maybe they'll go straight through and get here soon."

"The route they're going will take them away from us, but they can go down south and then back over to us. If they keep up, they should be here around Monday."

"Just like the Ouija revealed," Sarah said.

"Yeah, well, they have to deal with us and about a half dozen FBI agents that I called for." Warren said. "Rothberg and Doolard just made the FBI top most wanted list." He went back out to the living room.

Lois came in and said, "I should be going. I hope my board didn't upset you, Sarah."

"No, Lois. I'm just feeling the effects of the pregnancy. I may be a little off from now on."

"I was a monster when I was pregnant with my daughter. I actually felt sorry for my rotten bastard of an ex-husband. Good luck, Dave," she said and left.

They stood at the door watching to make sure Lois got to her car safely, then went back in the living room.

Gabe was resting on the couch with his head on Van Gogh, starting to fall asleep.

Sarah looked at Warren, "Sorry, but you and Walt are going to have to sleep on the air mattresses tonight. Gabe gets the guest room now."

"Why did I get so used to the bed last night? Oh, well," Warren laughed.

Dave went to Gabe, lifted him up and carried him to the bedroom. Warren followed to get his things out and took them back to the living room. Sarah prepared the bed and Dave set the boy down as they took off his clothes. They covered him and he was fast asleep. Van Gogh jumped up on the bed and settled down next to the boy. Sarah said to let the dog stay.

They went out of the room, leaving the door open. Back in the living room, Dave went to a closet and took out the air mattresses, handing them to Warren and Walt.

"You need to buy a pull-out bed couch. This is no way to treat guests," he said as he opened up the mattress. Dave handed him the pump and told him to blow.

An hour later, all was quiet in the house. Dave was holding Sarah closely in bed and they were talking.

"Gabe is a really polite boy, coming from such a bad life. Although he can be amazingly blunt, he's still polite about it. He's really grown," Sarah said.

"You know we still have to deal with his mother and her boyfriend coming," Dave said quietly. "From the murders they've committed, we need to be extra careful. I was thinking of sending you and Gabe out of town for a few days. Just until the dust settles."

"I'm not being run out of my home by two psycho morons. I'll stay here and hold my ground.

Gabe will not be harmed by anyone, including his mother. If we can call her that. I'm getting to like Gabe and I'm feeling sorry for him. He will never really know who his friends are, with all the wealth he's going to get. His parents are both useless and don't deserve him. I'd hate to see him end up in a bad foster home."

"There's not a lot we can do. The CPS has rules and he's going to be placed in a foster home. The only other alternative is that we become his foster parents." He paused to see what reaction Sarah would give.

She turned her head to him, looked him in the eyes and said, "I'd like that. Maybe it's the mother in me now, but I'd like that. We don't know what our baby will be, but it would be nice that our baby would have a big brother to look after him or her."

"I could talk to Millie Davis and see what we would need to do. It may change our life style a bit, having a boy in the house now."

"What life style? We sleep, get up, go to work, have dinner, when your schedule permits, and then watch TV before we go to bed again. The most excitement we've had was going to Las Vegas to get re-married."

Dave laughed softly. "Yes, we do have such a wild life style. I don't know if Gabe could keep up with us."

"Talk to Millie and see what she says. I'm still liking the idea of him staying with us. Besides, Van Gogh has already adopted him."

"Yeah, and I think Gabe has attached himself to Van Gogh. At least they can play with each other. You know there are no children out this way. I don't even know the neighbors, they're too far away to hang over the fence and chit-chat."

"The Millers are a nice couple. I met them once when Van Gogh ran off and I was looking for him. They have no children in the home since they are both in their seventies. Nice couple, though."

"Maybe we can adopt them as grandparents for Gabe," Dave said with a grin.

"They seemed very happy to be without children from what they told me. Nine children and they didn't want any more."

"Nine? They were busy, weren't they?"

"Yes, I think two children for us would be good. I could handle that. And Gabe is already out of diapers so that's no longer a problem."

"Yes, but he'll be a teenager on his next birthday, can you handle that?"

"You're already my big teenager. I can handle you, so I can handle him," she said with a laugh.

"Tomorrow is Halloween. I think I'll take you and Gabe out, give Mike a rest."

"Sure, you and Gabe can both wear your sheriff's uniforms and frighten people."

"As long as we don't arrest anyone. Now get to sleep. I think we'll be having a long day tomorrow."

Dave kissed her and they turned to spoon.

*

Chapter 22

Halloween.

The next morning, Warren and Walt were out fishing off the dock, as Sarah was making breakfast for Dave and Gabe. She was feeling a little better now until she almost burned the pancakes. Gabe was watching her struggle with the pan and suggested putting butter in the pan to keep the pancakes from sticking. She smiled and kissed the top of his head.

"Something smells halfway decent," Dave said as he came out to the kitchen.

"No comments from you. Sit and eat whatever I put in front of you. Gabe, have a seat."

The men sat as Sarah doled out the small pancakes on their plates. She set the syrup on the table as Dave and Gabe snickered at each other looking at the misshaped pancakes.

"Stop that, or you both can go without breakfast," she mugged.

"I'm for that," Dave said. Sarah whacked him lightly on the back of the head.

Warren came in the back door from the lake and into the dining area. "I just got a call from our friendly State Police. Seems Rothberg and Abby are still moving our way. They spotted them moving along Highway 18 near Hobart, but lost them around Maple Valley. The police think they hid along a side street. They're still watching for them. We haven't had a big manhunt like this in a long while. City, State and Federal cops all on the lookout."

"I'm surprised they're still in the state. With the killings they've been doing, I'd run north for the border of Canada. It's not that far," Dave said.

"Canada would send them back, they don't tolerate murderers. Besides, Rothberg and Abby have a goal," Warren said, subtly pointing to Gabe.

"Yes, and that's not a goal they're going to achieve," Sarah affirmed.

"Well, we have tomorrow to worry about it. Today is a big holiday. Trick or treating is in order," Dave said. "So, Gabe are you feeling good about going out tonight?"

The boy nodded his head as he ate the pancakes. "I'm happy," he said.

"Good. Warren, what are you dressing as?" Dave said, with a grin.

"A poor federal employee, wasting his life chasing bad people and getting little thanks," he said.

"Hey, we both got to visit the White House and received medals for saving the President. That was special."

"What did you do with your medal?" Warren asked Dave.

"Sarah hung it in the living room. I'm surprised you haven't seen it. Sarah mounted a spotlight on it."

"Well, I put mine in a drawer. Now I need to get back to the fish. Not many out there, did you chase them away?"

"They saw you coming and ran." Dave ate a couple bites of the pancakes and winked at Gabe.

An hour later the men were getting ready to go to the sheriff's station. Sarah was packing a lunch for Dave and handed it to him on his way out.

"I don't get a bag lunch?" Warren asked.

"You can eat candy out of the machine," Sarah said and kissed him on the cheek. On the way out Warren was calling to Dave that he got a kiss from Sarah.

"And that's all you'll ever get," Dave shot back.

They got to their vehicles and drove out. Sarah and Gabe watched them from the porch as they turned onto the highway.

"Do you worry about Dave getting hurt?" Gabe asked as they sat on the porch.

The question took Sarah by surprise and said, "Yes, I do, every day. But he could be hurt in a lot of professions. He's more susceptible to harm as a sheriff, but I know he can handle it." She was now thinking about what Dave and she were talking about in bed.

She looked at the boy and asked, "How would you feel about staying here a while longer?"

Gabe turned his head to her, smiled and asked, "Would you be my foster parents?"

Fatal Seance

She was surprised again by the boy's openness. "It was a thought Dave and I had. What would you think of that?"

"What about my parents?"

"Well, your father is going to be in prison for a very long time, a life sentence I heard, and your mother will also be going away for committing a few murders. They won't be around to take care of you."

"Do you want me to stay here?" he asked.

"Of course I do. I've grown to like you and I think Van Gogh does, too."

Gabe petted the dog, lounging next to him. "I like Van Gogh, too. What does that name mean?"

"It was the name of a famous painter of people and places, Vincent Van Gogh. I named him that name because my first husband was a painter."

"Did you divorce your first husband?"

Sarah could see the boy was going to be inquisitive. "No, Gabe. He died. Someone murdered him," she said, being honest.

"I'm sorry. Now you're married to Dave, so you're happy now?"

"Yes, I am, very much so. How would you like to go into town and have hamburgers for lunch?"

Gabe smiled and said he would.

~~*~~

"Good morning, Virgil. Did you get a good night's sleep?" Dave asked the man as he came in.

"I'm ready for anything," he said. "Now that the carnival is gone, we can all rest."

"Well, don't get too rested. We still have a pair of killers coming our way. They were last seen in Maple Valley."

"That's a long ways away. Are they heading here?" Virgil asked.

"It's what we figure," Warren said. "They're supposedly coming to get Gabe, and we need to stop them. They murdered two bikers last night. That brings the tally to five."

Fatal Seance

"Not very nice people, are they?" Virgil asked.

"No, Virgil, and they're very dangerous. So keep your head clear and be alert. Have you studied their rap sheets and photos?" Dave asked.

"I have. I got them burned into my memory. If I see them, I'll know them."

"Well, as much as we have to uphold the law, shoot first, ask questions later," Dave said and sat at his desk. Warren and Walt pulled up chairs and sat.

"Agent Stevens, does the FBI have plans for capturing the killers?" Virgil asked Warren.

"We don't know what's going to happen, so we are playing it by ear. Rothberg and Doolard keep changing their directions of travel, so we just have to watch for them. We figure the way they're going, if they are coming here, it should be sometime Monday."

"If they drove all the way, without stopping from Maple Valley, they could get here tomorrow," Virgil said.

"Yes, they could, if they drove straight through," Dave said. "They'd have to go near

Tacoma before Olympia, then here. So they'd have to stay off the radar or be stopped along the way."

"Hopefully," Warren said. "It would save us from stopping them."

"Actually, I'd like them to make it up here. Just to know we stopped them," Dave said.

"You love the action, don't you?" Warren laughed.

"I like to see things get tied up and finished."

"Well, I have the feeling you'll get your wish," Warren replied.

*

Chapter 23

It was a quiet day in Brinnon, so everyone had time to relax before the big assault. Dave, Warren, and Walt went to the Halfway House for lunch and talk.

Fatal Seance

"So did you enjoy your visit to Las Vegas?" Dave asked Warren.

"Other than hunting down bad cops, it was enjoyable. Have you heard from Jim Richards about the case?"

"I talked to him last week, he said they had everything gathered to close the case now and all the poisoned cosmetics have been destroyed."

"Good," Warren said as his cell phone buzzed. He answered and listened. He hung up and said, "They found Rothberg's car abandoned in Auburn. Looks like they commandeered another vehicle and continued. Now they don't know what they're driving. It's a theory but they probably are traveling on Highway 167 over to the 512, which will take them totally around Tacoma. Then they can go straight for Olympia."

"Then up here," Dave finished.

"Yep, so they may get here late tomorrow if they keep at it. Since the authorities don't know the vehicle they are driving, they can drive without worry."

"Unless they screw up again," Walt added. "Have you called for reinforcements?"

"I did this morning. The SAIC said he'd have more men out in the morning. Just to get settled in. But I don't think they'll have much time to settle before Rothberg rolls in."

"As long as they don't mess up Halloween, that's all I care about," Dave said. "Sarah and I had a talk last night about being foster parents for Gabe."

"Really? Do you think the two of you could handle a boy that old?"

"I don't see why not. He's smart and a good kid. Sarah would never let him get out of hand. She keeps me in line."

"Yes, she is the boss in your family," Warren laughed.

"She is," he replied. "Let's go back and wait. This is the part I hate."

They paid for the food and started to go out when they saw Sarah and Gabe coming up to the door.

"Did you decide to forgo making lunch and eat out?" Dave asked her.

"We came for a delicious hamburger and fries. A treat before we trick and treat tonight. Be sure to get home early enough to take us out, or we'll leave without you."

"There's still time before we need to go, so you can wait for me."

"Just be there," she warned and poked his stomach. She and Gabe went in and Dave took the men to his Rover.

"There's a big Halloween party at the VFW tonight, I hear. Maybe you two can go and pick up women," Dave said.

Warren looked at Dave and said, "No thank you, I've been to a couple VFW parties and there are no good looking, single women. The good ones are all married."

"Well, they have cheap drinks. You like that."

Warren laughed and said, "Walt, do you feel like hanging around the local VFW?"

"Sure, it might be interesting," Walt replied.

They arrived at the station and went in. Mike was standing at the counter, Virgil was at his desk.

"Hey, Mike. Ready to go watch for monsters and ghouls?"

"I'm not arresting any kids for begging," he replied.

"Good, we wouldn't have the room in the cell."

"I'll patrol the new subdivision. Easier to watch the people," Mike said.

"You may see me, Sarah and Gabe there. Good place to gather candy."

Virgil stood and said, "I'm going out to catch speeders, Dave."

"You do that, Virg. Make sure there are no children walking along the highway trick or treating."

"Too dangerous, I know. I'll make sure their parents are nearby," he said and left.

Mike went to his desk and sat. "Virgil said it was quiet overnight. There weren't any calls for Devil's Night. Nothing to report about vandalisms around the town."

"Not unless a bunch of seniors went out to TP a house. We don't have much trouble around here from the locals. It's the people who come into town who cause the trouble. Probably would be a good idea to patrol the campground, too. Just to be sure."

"Got it, chief. I'll do that later," Mike replied. "I'll go take a ride through the business district."

"Take your time, if I hear anything about our fugitives, I'll call and you come running."

Mike agreed, stood and went out.

Walt was working on his tablet and said, "Do you realize that the distance from Auburn to Brinnon in good traffic only takes about two hours to drive."

Dave looked at him, "Now that's not good to hear. Even in bad traffic and with frequent stops to hide from the police they still could still make it in about four hours at the outside."

"Yep," Walt said. "I calculated that with traffic flow around Olympia and avoiding road blocks by taking alternate routes, they could be here in four and a half hours."

"Damn, I hoped they wouldn't ruin Halloween," Dave said.

"Well, they know Gabe is in this town, but not exactly where he is. I'm sure they don't know he's staying with the sheriff," Warren said.

"I would rather they did. It might slow them down," Dave said. "They probably don't know he's surrounded by FBI either. Actually, I'd like some FBI personnel watching both Gabe and Sarah now. Just to be sure."

"The backup won't be in until tomorrow morning. If Rothberg and Doolard don't know where Gabe is exactly, they might hang around to watch for him. That would give us a little time before the Calvary rolls in."

"I think the three of us can take care of one man and one woman," Walt said.

"I like your confidence, Walt," Dave said. "I'm sure we could. But I'd rather be safe than sorry. Safety in numbers."

Warren was thinking, then said, "We need a plan. There's only one road coming up from Olympia, that's the 101. Dave, you stay with Sarah and Gabe for trick or treating. Walt and I will take Mike, or Virgil, and put a road block just below town on the highway, and watch for them."

Fatal Seance

"I'll leave it up to you, Warren, I want Gabe to have a good time trick or treating. Not worrying about his mother coming to try and take him. If you think it will work, go for it. I'll call Mike back in, he's more on the ball than Virgil. Let's get this organized."

~~*~~

Sarah and Gabe arrived back home after eating at the restaurant. Van Gogh needed to go out, so Sarah let Gabe take him. She knew Van Gogh would stay by Gabe, so she stood watching from the window as the boy and dog ran around the yard. She smiled at the thought of Gabe staying with them.

A few minutes later Gabe came in the house followed by Van Gogh. Sarah smiled and said he should start getting into his costume. They went into the guest room and Sarah had the clothes laid out. She went out of the room so Gabe could change, when she heard something at the front.

She went and saw it was Dave, alone. He came up to the door and in.

"Where are the others?" she asked.

"We need to talk," he said quietly.

*

Chapter 24

"What?" Sarah asked as Dave took her in the living room.

"Where's Gabe?" Dave asked.

"In his room with Van Gogh, getting into his costume."

"It looks like Rothberg and Abby may be up here tonight. Warren and Walt, along with Mike, are going to set up a road block on the 101 to see if they can divert them from coming into the town. I want Gabe to have a good Halloween without his mother screwing it up for him."

"Good, but what happens when they get here?"

"We have to take it one moment at a time. We have more FBI agents coming in the morning but that may be too late. It's up to Warren, Walt, Mike, Virgil and me to do this. As Walt said, if we can't handle one man and one woman, who can?"

"You have me with my gun, too. Don't forget that."

Dave kissed her and said, "I would never forget you. Now, let's get Gabe ready to go trick or treating."

They went to the guest room and found Gabe in his costume smiling at them. Van Gogh was standing next to him. He put on the hat and said, "I'm ready."

"You need a bag to collect the candy," Sarah said and went to the linen closet and took out a pillow case. She took it back to Gabe and gave it to him. "All set now. Shall we go?"

"It's still early, but it may be better to go while it's still light out," Dave said.

They went out to the car and before Dave started it, he called Warren. "Are you set up?"

Warren said into Dave's ear, "We're checking all cars coming into town. Mike has his cruiser running the flashers and Walt has the supervan flashing also. It looks impressive. If this doesn't give them second thoughts, I don't know what will."

"Good, we're heading out to go trick or treating, so we'll be away from the house. I left the back door unlocked if you need to get in. Watch for Van Gogh, he knows you, but he may give you a hard time coming in the back."

"Got it, call when you're finished and back." Warren hung up and Dave started the car. He said, "Here we go, Gabe, hope you get lots of candy."

They drove out to the new subdivision that was built in the last year on a nice piece of property west of the town. The place was three quarters occupied now, so there were enough houses to visit.

Dave parked his Range Rover at the mouth of the main street leading into the subdivision. There were already a number of children and parents walking by the houses, collecting candy. They could see Gabe was excited to go, so they started at the first house.

A woman came to the door and said, "Well, a little sheriff." Then she looked behind him and saw Dave in his uniform and she smiled. "Like father, like son," she called out. Dave smiled and waved.

"How's it feel to be a father now?" Sarah whispered to him.

Dave didn't say anything, he just grinned.

They walked around for about an hour as it was starting to get darker. They hit the last house and went back to the Rover. Dave stood outside the vehicle as Sarah and Gabe got in.

He pulled his cell phone and called Warren. "Anything happening?" he asked when Warren answered.

"They haven't come this way. Unless they were hiding in the trunk of a car. We didn't search every car completely. Keep an eye out, even though we haven't seen them."

Dave hung up and got in the car. He drove them back to the house as Gabe was digging into the bag of candy.

"Don't eat too much, I don't want you to get sick," Sarah warned the boy.

"Just the gummy ones," he replied, "for now."

Sarah smiled at Dave as they drove. They arrived back at the house just as Dave's cell phone buzzed. He answered it as Sarah and Gabe got out and headed to the house.

Caller ID said it was Mike. "Yeah, Mike, what's up?"

"I got a call from Virgil, he says Rothberg is in the Halfway House sitting at a table. Virgil spotted him from outside and doesn't think Rothberg saw him. He didn't see Doolard, but figured she may be in the restroom. Warren and Walt are following me there. Are you coming?"

Dave looked at the house and said, "I'll be there shortly. Do whatever Warren says." He got out and ran to the door calling for Sarah. She came to him and he said, "They've spotted the two of them, in the Halfway House. I'm going to help. Watch yourself." He turned to go back to his car and drove off.

Sarah took a breath and relaxed. She went into the kitchen to where Gabe had his candy spread out on the counter. Sarah took off her jacket and put it over the back of a dining chair. She lifted the .38 from its holster and set it on the kitchen counter, to adjust the belt. It was cutting into her waist from the weight of the gun. Gabe ran out to living room to find Van Gogh.

He yelled back to Sarah, "Where's Van Gogh?"

Fatal Seance

Sarah went out to the living room and looked around, she didn't see the dog. "Van Gogh!" she yelled. No response. Gabe went back into the hallway to the bedrooms looking for the dog.

"Van Gogh," Sarah yelled again.

Someone behind her said, "Stop yelling, I have a tremendous headache."

Sarah turned, startled when saw the woman standing with a gun on her. Sarah was over by the door to the back and her gun was in the kitchen. The woman came out from behind a wall in the living room, which separated the small study off the side.

"How did you get in here?" Sarah asked.

"You left your back door unlocked, not smart. But I guess living in the country, you don't get many intruders. I'm here for my son, where is he?"

"You're Abby Doolard, aren't you?"

"So, I guess you know about me. Then you know I like shooting people. I'll shoot you if I don't get my son."

"So you can keep him prisoner until you can collect this fortune, is that your plan?"

"It's not for you to know, nosy bitch. Now where is my son?"

Sarah wondered where Gabe was hiding. She hoped he was hiding.

"I haven't got all day, my boyfriend led your cops away so I could get Gabe. We'll have to move quickly to make our getaway. I told him I would wait for him down the road once I have the boy. Now stop wasting my time, where is he?" she screamed.

"I'm not giving him up. You can go to hell before I let you take him," Sarah said defiantly.

"No, you'll go to hell, bitch." She raised the gun up and said, "I can just kill you and find him myself. He's somewhere in the house. So say a prayer for your miserable life." She aimed the gun just as there was a loud gunshot. Doolard spun to see Gabe holding Sarah's gun. She gave a pained look and collapsed to the floor.

*

Chapter 25

Sarah ran to Gabe and took the gun. She stuck it in her belt and hugged the boy. He was too calm for what just happened.

"Are you alright?" she asked him, then she noticed tears in his eyes.

"I thought she was going to shoot you. I had to stop her. I'm sorry," he said, now hugging her.

"Don't be sorry, you saved my life. You are a real hero, Gabe. Worthy of that sheriff's uniform you have on," she replied holding him tighter. She took him in the kitchen and called Dave, explaining briefly what had happened. He told her he'd be right there.

Sarah had Gabe sit on a dining table chair. "Where's Van Gogh?" the boy asked. She turned and called again. She could hear a faint barking and went back to the utility room. She found Van Gogh in a closet and wondered how Doolard got him in there. Didn't matter, as long as the dog was safe. Van Gogh bounded out of the utility room and jumped on Gabe. The boy was laughing, which was a good sign.

Five minutes later, sirens were blaring as Dave pulled into the drive. He shut the car down and ran into the house.

"Are you all right?" he asked.

"I'm fine now." She led him to the living room and pointed to Doolard, now under a bed sheet that Sarah put over her body, so Gabe didn't have to look at her.

"Did you shoot her?" Dave asked.

"No, Gabe did." She explained everything in detail to him and he was amazed.

They went out to Gabe still in the kitchen with the dog. "How are you doing, champ?" Dave asked him.

"Better now that Sarah is safe," he replied.

"No problems with your mother being…well, dead?"

"No, she deserved it," he said quietly.

That gave Dave a slight chill that the boy was so accepting of what he had done.

"Okay, we can discuss this again later."

The front door opened and in came Warren and Walt. "What happened?" Warren asked.

Dave took them aside and explained the situation.

"Gabe may need therapy. Shooting his own mother, there has to be a precedent for that," Warren said.

"Well, he took it very well. He was more concerned for Sarah than his mother. She must have treated him real badly. Where's Rothberg?"

"Mike and Virgil are taking him to the station. He didn't put up much of a fight when we stormed the restaurant. Probably because he didn't have his gun. He left it in the car, he said. Not very bright indeed."

"We need to get this body out of here. I'll call the ME and have him take her away until it can be decided who gets her."

Warren was lifting the bed sheet. "I hate to say it, but you're going to need another new carpet again."

Sarah was standing nearby with Gabe. "That does it. I want hardwood floors in here now. No more carpets. Dave, call someone to arrange it."

Dave smiled and said, "Yes, dear."

~~*~~

The ME, Doc Norris, laughed and said, "You're making a regular shooting gallery out of this room. Fourth body now. I won't say it's a record but close."

"Just get her out of here, please. Warren will call his office and see what they want done with her. I'll let you know," Dave said.

Doc's men took the woman out to the van. Dave went to Gabe, sitting in the kitchen munching on candy with Sarah. She gave a sheepish grin to Dave and handed him a candy bar.

Fatal Seance

"Gabe, how did you know how to use a gun?" Dave asked him.

"My father used to take me out to my grandfather's woods and had me learn to shoot one of his handguns. He said you couldn't be a man if you couldn't shoot a gun."

"Well, there are different types of men who shoot guns. Bad men who kill, they're not real men, just cowards. Then there's law enforcement, they use guns to protect people."

"They're the good guys," Gabe said.

"Yes, they are. You shot the gun to protect Sarah, which was good, you saved her life. You were dressed like a sheriff, so you are a good guy. Remember that."

"I will," he said as he put the gummy bear in his mouth.

~~*~~

Monday morning, Dave had workers in to take out the soiled carpet and give an estimate for hardwood floors. The foreman said the floors under the carpet just need a good sanding and a couple coats of varnish and it would be an easy job.

That made Sarah happy and she took Gabe outside with Van Gogh to give the dog a run.

The FBI came in Sunday to take Doolard away from the morgue, Rothberg was being held for interrogation in the murder of Matthew Doolard and everything was returning to normal. Sarah came back in with the boy and dog. She said for Dave to come outside. He followed her out and found Millie Davis.

"From what I hear, you two have had a busy weekend. Is everything all right now?" she asked.

"It was a little hairy, but Gabe is safe from his mother now. His father has no chance of getting out of prison, so Gabe is alone now."

"Yes, and Sarah has told me that you two would like to become his foster parents."

"We would, very much so," Sarah said.

"I don't see any problems with it, but you'll have to fill out a number of forms to do so. Come into my office this week and I'll have the paperwork ready. You do know he has to be enrolled into a school?"

"Actually, Dave and I talked about that yesterday. I was homeschooled by my parents and we are thinking about that for Gabe. I called the K12.com people about what we would need to start and they are sending me the information."

"Well, that's fine, if you can do it."

"I don't have a lot on my schedule. I write books and I'll have a lot of free time to devote to Gabe's education."

"Good, come in and we'll fill out the papers."

She thanked them and left.

"Do you really want Gabe in our lives?" Sarah asked Dave.

"Are you chickening out now?" he replied.

"No, I just want to be sure. In seven or so months we'll have another child in the house. Our own child. Gabe will have to get used to being part of the family."

"I like Gabe, he's a good boy, and don't forget he saved your life."

184

Sarah grinned, "Plus he can shoot a gun, you'd like that."

"I'll admit, it's good to know."

"So we are good to have him in our lives?" Sarah asked.

"I'm ready to start," Dave said.

"Good," came a small voice from the porch. It was Gabe.

"How long have you been up there?" Dave asked.

"Ever since the nice lady left," he said, coyly.

"Listening in on people's conversations isn't nice," Sarah said.

"I was just standing here and you were talking. Should I have covered my ears?"

Sarah laughed and said, "No, how much did you hear?"

He grinned and said, "I heard that you wanted me to stay. That was all I needed to hear."

He came down from the porch and hugged Sarah, then Dave.

*

Chapter 26

"Okay, I have to go interrogate Rothberg to find out what happened," Dave said and kissed Sarah. He ruffled Gabe's hair and then went off to find Warren and Walt. They were in the back yard talking.

"So Rothberg stewed all day yesterday. Do you think he should be ready to talk?" Dave asked.

"We'll find out. Shall we go?" Warren said.

They drove over to the station and went in to find Rothberg quietly sitting in the cell. He wasn't very active looking, being rather meek now. Dave opened the cell to let the man out and take him to the interrogation room.

Rothberg stood and Dave went to put the cuffs on him, when Rothberg spun and hit Dave in the face with his elbow. Dave fell back as Rothberg reached down to grab his gun. Dave reached up and grabbed the man's shirt front and pulled him down. They were struggling when Warren came in to see what was going on.

"Hey," Warren yelled as Rothberg brought up Dave's gun and fired at Warren. He ducked quickly and jumped back out of the room. Rothberg held the gun to Dave's head and yelled out to Warren.

"I'll kill this bastard if you try to stop me!" he screamed. He pulled Dave up and they went out of the cell. Warren, Walt and Mike had their weapons trained on Rothberg. He kept behind Dave with the gun still on his head. "Move away now," he screamed.

"Take the shot, Warren, you know you can. Take him out," Dave said.

"Shut up. Shoot me, I shoot him. Want to take that risk?"

Warren smiled and said, "Sure." He pulled the trigger and hit Rothberg in the shoulder causing Rothberg to spin back enough for Dave to break loose and smash Rothberg in the face.

Dave grabbed his gun from Rothberg on his way down to the floor.

"You listened to me for once," Dave said to Warren.

"Glad to oblige. Shall we have medics look at him? I'm pretty sure I just grazed him."

They both examined the wound, it was just a graze. Dave called Mike to help patch him up.

They put the cuffs on him and took him to interrogation, cuffing him to the table. "Now asswipe, want to fill us in on what you and your bitch were doing?" Warren growled.

Rothberg sat staring into space. Warren slapped his face. The man yelled, "Hey! You can't do that!"

"Oh, I'm sorry, how's your wound doing?" Warren asked and squeezed the bandaged area. Rothberg screamed out loud.

"My, does that hurt?" Warren asked him.

"Don't!" Rothberg said softly. "Okay, I'll talk. I'm not good with pain."

"Good, now start from when you broke Doolard out of rehab."

Walt made sure his video recorders were working to record the testimony. Rothberg told them what they had already figured out about their crime spree across two states.

"How did you find out where Gabe was being held?" Dave asked.

"We went to social services and Abby identified herself as Gabe's mother. She told the woman that she wanted to visit her son."

"Who was that woman?" Dave asked knowing Millie would never have told them.

"Some clerk, I don't know who. She gave us a hard time, but Abby gave her a sob story and the woman finally gave in. She told us the address. I drove Abby up to the house and told her I would draw everyone away while she grabbed the kid. We arranged where to meet."

"Plausible, but poor planning. It didn't work, did it?" Warren said.

He didn't say anything.

"Okay, we have enough to convict," Warren said. "What with Klein's testimony and the video of the body dump. You, my friend, are going away for a long time."

Fatal Seance

They left him and went out. Dave said, "I'll call and have him transported to the county lockup. Then he'll be the state's problem. I'll have everything sent to the prosecutor's office."

An hour later, Rothberg was on his way to a jail cell in the county prison. Doolard's body was gone and Dave took a big breath of fresh air outside the station.

"Well, I guess we won't be needed any more. Walt and I will head back before we're missed, but it was definitely fun. I enjoy coming over here from Seattle to the country for fishing."

Dave watched them drive off and was feeling empty now. The crime wave was over and his friends had left. Now he had to build a life with Gabe. He told Mike that he was going home and left.

He got to his house and saw Sarah standing out front with Gabe and Van Gogh. He pulled in, parked and Sarah went to him.

"I got a call from Millie. She needs to see us in her office."

"All of us?" Dave asked.

"That's what she said," Sarah replied.

"Okay, gather the boy and let's go."

Dave was concerned now as to why Millie was calling them in so quickly. He drove them to the county building and around to the CPS shelter next door. They found Millie in her office.

"Thank you for coming. I'm sorry for the short notice, but it was important," Millie said.

Now Dave was worried.

"I finally got the files from CPS in Salem, Oregon for Gabe's being housed there. It's standard procedure to locate all living relatives before placing a child in a home, to avoid problems later if a close family member wants to claim custody of the child. It seems Gabe does still have a close relative."

"Who?" Sarah asked.

"His grandmother on his father's side. She divorced Gabe's grandfather many years ago and moved away. She remarried and is living in Seattle now. I had to call, by law, to let her know the boy is here. Since Salem CPS never called her because the mother was still living, she didn't know where the boy was. She wants to see the boy, so she is coming over today to visit. I didn't ask her about whether she wants custody of the boy or not, I'll wait until she gets here."

Now both Sarah and Dave were worried. "What if she wants to take Gabe?" Sarah asked.

"She has a legal right to obtain custody if she wants to. I'm hoping she doesn't."

Gabe looked up to Sarah and said, "Do I have to go with her? I don't even know her."

"Let's take it one step at time, Gabe." Dave said. "When will she be here?"

"She left just after I called her, or so she said she would. She should be here shortly."

They had nothing more to say and just waited in the hallway for the woman. About forty minutes later, an older woman came in with a younger man escorting her. Millie saw them and went to her. "Mrs. Kepler?" she asked.

The woman said she was and followed Millie to her office. Millie waved to Dave and Sarah to come in. The young man waited outside of the office. They all sat.

Mrs. Kepler, this is Sheriff Dave Chandler and his wife Sarah. This young man is Gabe Doolard, your grandson."

Gabe was holding on to Sarah's hand as the woman said hello to the boy.

"Hello, ma'am," Gabe said back.

"Sheriff Chandler and his wife have requested custody as foster parents for Gabe. This was started while your daughter-in-law was still alive. She's not now, so we need to decide custody of Gabe, since you have been notified."

*

Chapter 27

"What happened to my daughter-in-law?" Mrs. Kepler asked.

Dave spoke up. "Mrs. Kepler, she was a wanted woman for murdering a number of people. She was shot while trying to kidnap Gabe. It's a long, sordid story that I can share later, if you want."

"Oh goodness, no. I never liked that woman. She just had a mean streak that bothered me. Good riddance, I say. I'm sorry, Gabe, I know she was your mother."

"It's okay," Gabe said.

"Sheriff, you and your wife want to be foster parents to my grandson. Can you provide him with a steady life?' she asked.

"We've gotten to enjoy having him since we've been taking care of him. He has fit right in with us. Even our dog has attached himself to Gabe. My wife has also contacted someone about schooling for him. This was before we knew about you."

"You do know about the money he will inherit when he turns twenty-one?"

"I thought it was sixteen, from what Gabe said?" Dave said. "And we aren't interested in the money. It's Gabe we want to take care of."

"No, not sixteen. I remember when I was divorcing Hiram, Gabe's grandfather. He said he'd be damned if I ever saw a penny. It was all going to Gabe, when he turned twenty-one. I didn't care who got the money, it was what caused our divorce. He was so wrapped up in wealth, he didn't care about his family. The only reason he gave it to Gabe was to cut our boys out."

"I don't want the money," Gabe said.

"Well, it's up to you what you do with it, Gabe. Just decide wisely." The woman paused. "I'm old and there's no way I could take care of a young child. The young man with me is my husband's son and he takes care of me. It wouldn't be fair for Gabe to live in a house with a doddering old woman. My stepson is gay so he's not interested in children at the moment. I think that the sheriff and his wife would be best for Gabe," she said to Millie.

Dave took a silent breath and felt good. Sarah held Gabe's hand tighter.

"I just wanted to see my grandson, since I have no family left other than my two sons. One of whom is in prison, the other is off somewhere."

Dave didn't want to tell her he was dead, maybe later.

"So, Miss Davis, let these nice people take care of him. But I insist that he come visit me often. Is that acceptable to everyone?"

They all agreed. Gabe was grinning widely.

He stood and went to the woman, giving her a hug. "Thank you, grandma," he said softly, she squeezed him and then let him go.

"Well, it's a long ride back to Seattle. I'm not used to being out in the car, so I think I'll be going." She stood, then everyone got up. "It's good to meet you, Sheriff, and Sarah. Take good care of my grandson."

"We will," Sarah replied, "and we will bring him to visit you often."

"Good." She left the office and the young man escorted her out of the building.

They turned to Millie as she said, "Shall we start the paperwork?"

A while later they arrived back at the house. Gabe was running around the yard with Van Gogh, as Dave and Sarah sat on the porch watching them.

"Have you told Gabe about the baby yet?" Dave asked.

"We had a talk about it yesterday while he and I sat by the lake. He's excited to have a little brother or sister."

"Well, we'll have a good little family, won't we?" Dave said.

"You bet. You know that Gabe will remember Halloween as the night he shot his mother," Sarah said.

"I think he'll remember it as the night he saved you." Dave replied.

"I like that much better," she said.

"What about the gypsy's vision?"

"I thought about that," she replied. "When she came to the house, she was warning us that I could lose a child, if we weren't careful. Then she said the child would save himself and someone close to him. Gabe saved me and himself from his mother by shooting her. So, I guess the old woman was very close to the truth. But I'm not saying I believe in fortune telling and séances."

"Of course not," Dave said and smiled, as they sat happily watching Gabe and the dog running around chasing squirrels.

THE END

~~*~~

Special Peek at a New Book

The following is a chapter from a book that may become a new series. So far the working title of this book is "Gus Mackie and the Hot Tamale", but it could change. Here is the first chapter for you to read since it's still a work in progress.

Chapter 1

I just about fell back in my desk chair, falling asleep. It was a boring, dusky, rain-soaked Tuesday and I had no clients coming through my door.

I'm Gus Mackie, private dick and super snooper for hire. Unfortunately, no one was hiring me right now, and my bank was going to foreclose on my wallet. Not that I cared. I lived in the back of my office that was a gift from a thankful client, one who I spared from an expensive divorce. I proved his wife was screwing his servants.

His wife, Else, was hopping from bed to bed in his palatial mansion in the swanky neighborhood of Grosse Pointe, Michigan. Just down the street from the Fords of auto fame. He was your basic slum lord and probably was dealing drugs on the side, but he was good to me, after I exposed his wife for the cheating slut she was. He probably also had mob ties, which I never asked about and never will. I liked living, if you could call this living.

My office was located on the fourth floor of the building, in a crappy neighborhood located in the nicest slum of Detroit. It wasn't the best I could get, but it was rent free. As long as Kenny Grabowski was happy with me, so I tried not to piss him off. I couldn't afford to go anywhere else.

I had a small amount of cash hidden in a can of beans that I bought at Bed, Bath and Beyond, for hiding your valuables. The top screwed off and you could put money or jewelry into it and put it on a shelf.

Of course, it looked stupid. One can of beans alone on a shelf. If that didn't give it away, well, criminals had gotten stupider.

I stared at the picture of the latest Playmate of the Month that I hastily taped up on my wall. The only decoration I had. She was enticing, but sex was something I hadn't indulged in for a long time. I wasn't the Tom Selleck, private investigator, type of detective. So women weren't beating down my door to pillage and rape me. I was more like Peter Falk in Columbo, without the fake right eye.

Fatal Seance

I was the sole proprietor of my business, and I couldn't afford a secretary. Didn't need one, since I had very few people coming in to hire me. Maybe if I advertised, I could build up business. Unfortunately, advertising cost bucks, which I didn't have.

I worked by word of mouth. Mostly divorce lawyers who would hire me occasionally to spy on unfaithful spouses. Just about every P.I. that I knew of chased after cheating spouses. It was a lucrative business, since all spouses cheat at one time or another. Unfortunately, it wasn't lucrative enough for me. I had three cases in the last month, enough to buy food and pay the utilities. Not enough to get drunk on, though.

My door opened and in came a strangely well-groomed man, fifties and wearing a hat that old men wore. I think they call it a pork pie. Why it was called that, I didn't know, or care. It didn't look like it went with his tailored suit, but I'm not a fashion maven myself.

"Morning. May I help you?" I started the conversation.

"Are you Gus Markie?" he asked.

"No, I'm Gus Mackie, P.I., but sometimes I'm confused with Gus Markie. What can I do for you?" I asked, hoping he needed someone followed.

"I need someone followed."

Bingo. I leaned forward and said, "You came to the right place, please have a seat." I motioned him to the chair in front of my desk, and he sat after dusting the chair with a handkerchief.

I was slightly offended. I dusted my office every day, mostly out of boredom. But, hopefully, he was going to be a paying client, so I let him dust away. Maybe I would let him dust the rest of the office, but I didn't want to push my luck.

"Who do you want me to follow, Mr. – um?"

"Glocksteiner, Hans Glocksteiner. I own Glocksteiner Antiques downtown. We sell antiques and auction off estates."

"Okay, Mr. Glocksteiner, who is it you want followed?"

"My secretary, I think she's cheating on me."

"I see. What makes you think she's cheating on you?"

"I just have the feeling. She's not meeting with me anymore when I arrange for a hotel room to have our trysts."

"Hotel room? You meet in hotels? Why?" I asked, figuring I knew what he was going to say.

"So my wife doesn't find out, of course."

Another bingo.

"Okay, so you are stepping out on your wife and you want me to find out if your mistress is stepping out on you, am I correct?" I asked.

"I'm not fond of the term, 'mistress'. We are in love and I want to be sure she is totally faithful before I divorce my wife," he said with a haughty air.

"Okay, I understand now. I'll need details on where I can find her and something to go on for her activities. Do you want to discuss my fees?"

"Of course." He looked around my office, probably figuring from the lack of furniture and décor, I came cheaply.

"My fee is one hundred dollars a day while on the case, plus expenses. I'll provide you with receipts for expenses. There's a two hundred dollar retainer to start."

"Not as bad as I thought, so when can you start?"

"When do you want me to start?"

"As soon as possible. I arranged to meet her in the Wittier Hotel tonight but she said she had plans. I asked what and she got defensive. So I didn't push the issue. You can start tonight."

"Fine." I pushed the writing pad to him and told him to write down everything about her. He started to write as I sat back thinking that I could finally buy a six pack of beer.

He was gone after five minutes of writing and I had two hundred dollars of his cash. He had a big wad of bills that he pulled out of his jacket. I thought of running down the fire escape and mugging him from behind, but he was a client and I charged by the day. I might make this one last a week. Mugging just the same.

I went over to my bean can and put one hundred of the two in the can. I set it back on the shelf and thought about buying a few more cans of real food. Just to hide the fake can.

Fatal Seance

I went to my desk and called the one good friend I had in the city, Bernie Longmire. He was a Native-American Sioux and I've known him since the Army. We both served in Germany and he was the only person to make friends with me. I didn't play nice with people, but he didn't care. We were both in the Military Police and he tolerated me. Any person who could put up with me was okay in my book.

He was now a mid-grade detective with the Detroit Police and would help me when he could. He answered his phone when I called and said, "What now, Gus?"

I hated caller ID, it spoiled the surprise. "I'm just checking in to see if you're still alive."

"Horse manure, you want something. What?" he replied, in that monotone way he spoke.

"I just want a background check on a guy. Simple."

"Nothing is simple with you. Give me the facts." He knew me too well.

*

Continued in the book…

Bob Moats

The Jim Richards books by Bob Moats
(In series order)

Classmate Murders
Vegas Showgirl Murders
Dominatrix Murders
Mistress Murders
Bridezilla Murders
Magic Murders
Strip Club Murders
Made-for-TV Murders
Mystery Cruise Murders
Talk Show Murders
Sin City Murders
Black Widow Murders
Vegas Vigilante Murders
Area 51 Murders
Mortuary Murders
Hypnotic Murders
Sunshine State Murders
Blue Suede Murders
Honky Tonk Murders
Dark Carnival Murders
Lipstick Murders
Pasta Murders
Talent Show Murders
Shyster Murders
Campground Murders
Network Murders
Reunion Murders
Big Apple Murders
Kennel Murders
Trick or Treat Murders
Santa Murders
Wiseguy Murders
Toxic Murders

For a preview or where to purchase a book, go to
http://murdernovels.com

Jim Richards Family of Readers

Thanks to the following people who are now part of the Jim Richards Family of Readers. They have read a book or more and enjoyed them. They all volunteered to be included in the list. If you are a fan of the books, send me your full name and you will be included in future books. Send your name to murdernovels@bobmoats.com to be added here and on the website.

* Achim Feifel * Al Norris * Alex Wheatley * Alexandra Delporte-Wilkinson * Amy Tapia * Andrea Bryan * Anne Shepherd * Arianda Sugar * Arlene Markowski * Ashley Augustus * Audra Hall * Barbara Hughes * Barbara Sammons * Barbara Schuler * Barbara Zirger * Beth Donohue Plenskofski * Beth Rosin * Betsy Childress * Beth Gibson * Bill Sandy * Bill Tornquist * Billie-Jo Collie * Boni J Rychener * Candace Larson * Carl Bishopric * Carla Lewis * Carole Henderson * Carolyn Conroy * Carolyn Riddle-Linington * Casey Moats * Cassy Bailey * Cathie Turner * Chad Hudson * Charlie Meier * Charlotte L Duran * Cheryl L. Everett * Cindy Ackley Nunn * Cindy Valstad * Connie Bancroft * Corinne Kay O'Daniel * Dana Robbins Chuchran * Dana Wichita * Daniel Kalus * Danielle Monique * Darren Heald * Dave Travers * David Wilkinson * DeAnn Jannereth * Deanna Miller * Deb Breuker Balbo * Debbie Carter * Debbie White * Deborah Fartuch * Deborah Gauze * Deborah Sullivan * Dee King * Denise Freeman * Diana Carver * Dixie Beck * Donna Gould * Donna Thompson * Donny Minter * Doris Kight * Eddie Moore * Eric Walters * Felicia Annette Bradfield * Francine

Bob Moats

Menor * Gail Chesney * Georgiann Minster * George Conner * Greg Colucci * Hayley Rankin * Harold Garcia * Heidi Arnold * Irma Ranee Coy * Jacqueline Moss * Jan Kimball * Janet Lawson * Janice Schneider * Janice Spoor * Jennifer Redmond * Jerry Dornak * Jessica Keown-Belous * Jim Beck * Jo Boguslaw * Jo Turner * Joanne Marie Turner * John Gross * John Peiffer * John Wisbiski * Joseph Wauro * Joyce Stacy * Joyce Trifiletti * Judy Franklin * Judy Travers * Judy Padgett * Julie Heath * Junnahvee Benson * Justin Moats * Karen Dahl * Karen Grams * Karen Higham * Karen Kaiser * Karen Meinburg Richwine * Karen Kirkman Parker * Karin Hawkins * Karin Vasvari * Kathleen Donohue Roesing * Kathleen Riddle-Wolfe * Kathy Hinds Moore * Kathy Jones * Kathy Mitchell * Katie Benzler * Kay Burns * Kelly Garcia * Ken Boggs * Keota Rodriguez * Kiera Mccarthy * Kim Estes * Kimberley May * Kitty Stolle * Kristie Sciler * Kirsty Stanton * LaLonnie Scallen * Larry Morris * Leann Parr * Lenora Scales * Leslie Marie Jackson * Linda Bartley Florence * Linda Forester * Linda Ingle Cox * Linda Kennerö * Linda Magill * Lisa Bower * Lisa Keller * Liz Gibson * Lorraine Wiman * Loretta Alexander * Lynda Bowles * Lynette Lawrance * LuAnn Louttit * Manny Rothman * Marcia Gibson DeWitt * Marie Calder * Marlene Bryan * MaryLouise Kramp * Mary Lynn Gross * Megan Atkins * Meghan Hyden * Melissa Wescoat * Melody Cannavan * Michael Carruthers * Michael Dinkens * Michael Vannoy * Michelle Burns-Mitchell * Michelle Pilcher * Micki Potter * Mike Moats * Mimi Baur * Myrna Hecht * Nadine Sutton * Nancy Ellen Sayre * Natalie Quine * Neena Martin * O'Della Wilson * Pat Pollington * Pat Rohn * Patricia Jarmon * Patricia C Trezza * Patrick Barry * Paul Lawrance * Peggy Davis * Phyllis Bassett * Raylene Matheny * Rebecca Collins Besner * Renee

Fatal Seance

Brumley * Reta Hanna * Reta Moats * Robert Lenski * Roberta Meister * Roberta Navarro-Harder * Sally Berneathy * Sally Hubler * Sara Swope * Sarah Santos * Satka Nikc * Sharon E. Edwards * Sharon Mangini * Sharon McMillon * Sheena Rawl * Sherry Amstutz * Sherry Tull * Shirley Alvarez * Shirley Davies * Shirley Williams * Stacie Rowe * Stephanie Conner * Steve Cullen * Susan Haughton * Susan Hesse Adams * Susan Salomon * Suzan K Chase * Taisha Cullum * Tamara Moore * Tammy Castleberry * Tammy Lynn Wood * Ted Murphy * Terri Atkins * Terri Creech * Terry Raab * Tonia Rachael Riggs-Williams * Tonya Mann * Travis Fleury-Lopez * Twyla Gawlas * Val Brooks * Walt Munsel * Yvonne Isakson

Thank you to all these wonderful people.

Thank you for purchasing this book. I hope you enjoy it as much as I enjoyed writing it for my faithful readers. Please feel free to email me to tell me what you thought about my stories. I love hearing from the readers. I can be reached at murdernovels@bobmoats.com thanks again!

*